Journalist,

sonality, Fi

seven bestse

On the Road, Galactic Girl, From Here to Virginity and *In Depth.*

Also in Arrow by Fiona Richmond

In Depth
On the Road
Galactic Girl

THE GOOD, THE BAD AND THE BEAUTIFUL

Fiona Richmond

ARROW BOOKS

Arrow Books Limited
17-21 Conway Street, London W1P 6JD

An imprint of the Hutchinson Publishing Group

London Melbourne Sydney Auckland
Johannesburg and agencies throughout the world

First published by Star 1980
Arrow edition 1983
Reprinted 1985

Printed and bound in Great Britain by
Anchor Brendon Ltd, Tiptree, Essex

ISBN 0 09 932830 5

This book has been made more difficult by Georgina, Boscombe and Kevan Sheehan.

CONTENTS

Chapter One

DAIRY BOX COCKS

Meanwhile, hell could not have been hotter than that high noon in Gold Dust – the oppressive heat shimmered in a heavy haze. It hung around on street corners; hid in lurking clouds like an angry alleycat ready to pounce on any unsuspecting venturer. There was just no escape from its penetrating rays. Everything hung limp and languid – except at Lurex Tex's fun parlour.

Through an open upstairs window of the sprawling cathouse, the monotonous creak, creak, creak of bedsprings could be heard as Tex plied her trade. She never missed a trick. Even now, in this baking heat, she was lying under the body of some cowpoke from somewhere. From her horizontal position, Lurex Tex watched the progress of a fly as, unseeingly, it crawled its way into a gecko's salivating mouth. With a flick of a leathery head, the lizard snapped up the insect in one neat gobble.

The gnarled face above Tex was not unlike that of the lizard; lined from over-exposure to the hot dusty elements of the American mid-West. Small droplets of sweat formed on the cowboy's brow and began to drip like a leaky faucet onto Tex's upturned countenance. He ground away, bent solely on his own pleasure. Tex didn't mind. Men. She didn't love them. She was simply hung-up on cocks. Small ones, fat ones, long ones, lopsided ones. Cocks were her business. She was more a cockomaniac than a nymphomaniac. She gave hardly a thought to the man behind the weapon; but concentrated all her attentions on the silken shaft of much-stained steel. These she used to transport her from the seedy surroundings into a heaven-from-hell. Lurex Tex hugged the cock to herself, a delicious secret she wasn't going to share with anyone. The cowboy was in full gallop. Tex took her time, so expert was she at controlling her own coming. So deft was she at this bronco riding, that she was able to catch up and overtake any horseman at any time. With a grunt, the cowboy unloaded his sharpshooter into the middle of her target. Tex answered this bang with an explosion of her own. She had come. And the railroad was coming . . .

Minutes later, the cowboy pulled on his trousers, holstered up and blew.

Lurex Tex, fresh out of clients, sat up in bed and laughed. She was the gecko and they were the flies – she proved it every time. To think she got paid for being on the receiving end of a non-stop stream of Dairy Box cocks. She sank back onto the mattress and almost disappeared into the soft furnishings. On the old chest beside the bed was a neat pile of notes. One dollar notes, five dollar notes and ten dollar notes. Tex glanced across at the dusty wooden surface. She smiled with satisfaction as her eyes lit on the money.

'Not bad for a quiet morning's work in Gold Dust,' she mused.

Tex stretched her legs. She could still feel the weight of the hard, unyielding body that had so recently lain on top of her. Her huge mane of coarse blonde hair hung down over one ear in a curious loop. Her almond eyes slanted upwards at the corners, giving her a strange Asian look. She had ferociously plucked her brows into high arches, which emphasised her heavily-lashed eyes. Her pert nose pointed to her over-sticked lips. All that this gal had was over-underlined; cheeks too rouged and her eyes too shaded. The skin under her chin was beginning to sag perceptibly, from too much bad living and good liquor. Her body was faring better in this battle of time. Good shapely breasts topped by nipple halos the size of saucers stood proudly up from a sea of smooth cream flesh. A neat waist and solid child-bearing hips tapered off into long, lissome legs.

Tex stroked herself and surveyed her thick pubic thatch. She couldn't resist the pull of her own pussy. Her finger plunged into the hot melting pot. Its lips unfolded. They were fat and juicy, from the pollen left by the big angry bee. What had he looked like? Tex frowned. She had no idea. He'd smelt of her lavender soap and leather. She always made them wash in fresh-scented water, which she kept in her tasteful jug and basin on the dressing table. Even she did not want a man who smelt like a horse. She shuddered and relived the moment of penetration.

Outside, in the one street the town boasted, not a stick stirred. The occasional old man, an occasional old hat pulled down over his occasional old head, dozed on an occasional old chair in an occasional old doorway. No one saw the small cloud of dust approaching from the west. As the powder puff drew closer, it became recognisable as two figures on horseback – one vertical and one horizontal.

The horses hooves bit into the arid dirt-track, clopping their way past the first wooden shack marking the beginning of town. Gold Dust had seen better days. This one-eyed, one-horse, one-cock town had been the very centre of a frenetic goldrush ten years before. Still the myth of the 'Mine of Solid Gold Nuggets' hung in the steamy air. But most real prospectors had long since gone. And with them the prosperity that the now-faded town, and Tex, had so enjoyed. All that was left were two rows of ramshackle structures, fringing the wide deeply-rutted main street.

Although interest in the fabled gold-filled mine had so waned, Tex still clung to her own fantasy. Somewhere, near her Gold Dust home, she was convinced that the mine lay waiting for her. Somewhere in the Superstition Mountains, which brooded on the horizon, lay the mine. The mine was reputed to be so filled with gold that, were the walls tapped with a hammer, nuggets would shower down like golden rain. But the secret of the mine's whereabouts was well guarded by passing time. Many people lost life, limb and cock in their vain search for veins. Rumours abounded of the seam of gold as high as a cliff, from which shovels of pure gold could be dug.

One legend had it that the Apaches showed a European discoverer a place where he could pluck gold like apples from a tree. They'd led him there blindfold and he had taken away as much as he could carry. Later, when he returned with a group of fellow prospectors, they had all been butchered by the Indians. All other expeditions in search of the mine had ended in death. Heads had fallen and balls had rolled. The Apaches believed that the mine would continue to bring bad luck and destruction to any who found it. So they set about stopping any intrusions. They did a tribal rain dance and, while the medicine man was in the throes of his magic, attempting to bring a flood, someone tripped him up and an earthquake shortly followed; thus the mine's secret was hidden for ever and a day.

The two horsemen rode on. By now they had overshot Gold Dust and had to do a one hundred and eighty degree turn. As they re-entered the town from the east, a laugh was heard. This was shortly followed by another laugh. In no time, great peals of irregular mirth rang out from all the houses like bells gone mad. Gold Dust was waking from its mid-afternoon slumbers! The rider of the first horse – the vertical one – was instantly recognisable even to the sleepy bleary-eyed inhabitants of this hillbilly town. A large black sombrero kept his thin, almost elfin face in a shadow. A wisp of blue smoke snuck out from under the brim. A long thin dark rod of tobacco sat on his lower lip. Despite the heat of the day, the rest of him was shrouded in a massive brown-fringed poncho. Black pencil-thin trousers were tucked into fancy hand-stitched boots with mule-ears. The imposing man's one concession to colour was the bright yellow ornamental bandana that protected his neck from the desert sun. His silver dress spurs sent morse-code messages in the sunlight. He sat upon his mount straight-backed and rode with an elegant nonchalance. This wild-west Victorian weirdo was not amused or moved by the town's babblings. Nothing moved The-Man-With-No-Voice. The laughter was not directed at him, however, but at the poor unfortunate slung over the horse behind him.

'To be tied across your very own saddle is humiliating enough,' thought Big Nose Joe, 'but to be bare-arsed as well is a total disgrace.'

The whole town was wide awake now and even Tex had left her bed and was at her boudoir window displaying her pert half-naked breasts to the newcomers. She giggled.

'Big nose, big cock – I wonder if it's true,' she quipped over her shoulder to the maid.

She leant out of the window in an attempt to verify the old wives' tale but all she caught a glimpse of was the full moon of Joe's arse, bobbing, bright red from its sudden prolonged exposure to sunlight. Joe muttered curses mainly, as the saddle bit into his bare flesh in a most uncomfortable fashion.

This was sure no way for a great gun-slinging dude to meet his end, thought saddle-sore Joe. Poor Joe; his end was very much in view that day – much to the delight of the townsfolk of Gold Dust.

The-Man-With-No-Voice looked neither to the right nor to the left. He headed his horse straight for the sheriff's office, tied the beasts – all three of them – to the rail and made for the tumbledown shack that served both as jail and office. Inside it was cool and gloomy. The sheriff was stirring from his afternoon siesta. His feet still rested on what served as his desk, as he allowed himself the luxury of a little yawn. In mid-stretch, he caught sight of his visitor and with surprising speed for one so thick with sleep, leapt to his feet. In his haste, his pendulous jinglebobs got caught in the tattered seam of his batwings. He fell heavily to the floor and sat on his spurs, his torn chaps falling with him. From his pain and pileful position, the yiddisher sheriff, Hymie Rosen, (he'd long ago dropped the Berg) croaked:

'What y'all got there, No-Voice?'

No-Voice looked disdainfully down at the mess on the floor that posed as a sheriff and thought to himself: 'If I had a nose like that, I wouldn't underline it with a moustache.'

The sombre bounty-hunter put out a leather-gloved hand in an attempt to raise the fallen lawman. Once the large lump was on its feet, No-Voice indicated the door with a jerk of his thumb. The other hand formed itself into a Victory salute. The price of the man with the blistered arse was two thousand dollars.

The sheriff ducked out of the doorway and found himself nose-to-arse with Joe. He let out a chuckle that travelled up the hollow of Joe's bottom. Hymie left the bare-faced cheek and shambled round to study the mug. Sure enough, it was the Bum-Bandit with two grand on his head. Sheriff Rosen came back into his counting house and started counting out his money in a most penny-pinching fashion.

'Sure beats me how you always get yer man and bring him in alive and naked as day he was born. There are never no extra holes in your victims,' trilled Rosen.

The bounty-hunter took the crisp wad of notes, tipped his hat in a gesture of thanks and left without a word – not at all unusual for The-Man-With-No-Voice!

The good and bad people of Gold Dust stopped laughing as the hunter departed. Fear had taken the place of their amusement. They stepped back out of the sunlit sidewalks into dark doorways, as the shadow of death passed them by. They always associated No-Voice with death, yet, like Wyatt Earp, he had never fired a single shot. His victims were always brought to justice the same way; naked and upon their mounts! No-Voice was soon a dot of dust in the distance. The townspeople crowded Big Nose, and men began poking fun and sticks at his privates, as the sheriff cut him loose. Prim bonneted women pretended to put their hands over their eyes, but secretly peeked through their fingers at his donkey-like dong.

A raucous yell cut through the hubbub of voices. 'My, my, Big Nose, it's true what they say,' screeched Tex. 'If you ever get outta jail, just you bring yer Western Wonder along over to my place and I'll give yer a ride fer nothin'.'

The men laughed at lurid Lurex. The women composed their features into expressions of extreme distaste, while their fannies twitched with base excitement at the penile display on the main street.

'Prissy cows,' shrieked Tex and slammed down her window.

The sight of Big Nose's great white wonder had made her feel randy. She flopped on the bed and a cloud of black lace billowed over her. She was wearing her fucking best. A hand quickly burrowed its way through the acres of negligee and within seconds, she had her pussy cupped carefully in her grasp. Fingers rubbed up and down, delicately toying with the red-hot button. She traced around and around the many folds, drawing her knees up and apart as she did so. She pressed her rump deep into the mattress and moved it around. Her fingers worked across, while her plump lips rotated. The cross friction soon had her clit tingling. A deep ache started way down inside her. She closed her eyes and Big Nose's giant cock sprang erect into view. She had to have something to fill the need which stirred within. First one finger, then two were sucked up her oily well. With her thumb, she massaged her hard hairy mound. Moisture was creeping onto her finger. She felt her cheeks glow and the warmth spread around her body. That awesome tingle, which had started at the tip of her lips, now began to travel. Her digits moved faster, getting wetter all the time. She was juiced up, ready to burst.

'Big nose, big cock,' she moaned to herself.

Her bud felt like molten gold. And the goldrush had begun. The flood burst its bank, her eyes flickered and closed. 'Big Nose, big cock, big cock, big cock, big . . .'

Her legs flattened out. Her body heaved. The spasm started to grip her. She heard her breath coming in rasps, as the urge grew out of all proportions and gave way to that wonderful secret lovely guilty feeling of giving yourself the utmost in sex. Full of liquid fire, she came quietly and alone. And the railroad was coming . . .

Back at the jail, Big Nose was experiencing a climax of a different kind. It was the first time he'd been caught on the job. But at least he was now safe in jail. He'd never thought that he'd feel easier inside such an establishment but it sure was a relief job to be tucked safely away from the cries of derision, peering eyes and that loud-mouth Lurex Tex. Big Nose Joe was not the sort of man you took the piss out of. He was a rough, tough gambling man. At this moment, however, he stood in a position of ridicule.

He was goodlooking in a rugged sort of way but this handsome, butch figure did nothing to lawman Rosen. In fact Hymie did nothing to hide his amusement at the outlaw spectacle. He grinned in glee right into Joe's private's. He was a very short sheriff!

'Well, I'll be hanged,' he drawled, scratching his bullet-shaped head, 'how did you get yourself in a fix like this?'

The next piece of conversation was drowned by a passing 747.

'I . . . er . . . umm . . .' Big Nose stammered.

He blushed the colour of a Californian sunset. The sheriff noticed with interest that every part of his body turned a bright puce. Not the seventh wonder of the world – but close! Big Nose shuffled his feet and studied them intently. His corns stuck out like shoots from an old potato. But he was still handsome – he had to be, otherwise it would ruin the plot . . .

'Gimme some clothes,' said Big Nose.

Covering the prisoner with his gun, Hymie attempted to cut the ropes at his prisoner's wrist. Blood welled from the sheriff's open veins and he fell in a gory heap on the floor. Big Nose could hardly believe his luck. The whole thing does tax one's credulity. However, as it happened, Hymie's twin brother, Hermie, who stood in when Hymie was on his hols in Tucson, arrived through the front door of the jail to take over the job permanently.

Hermie tackled the ropes around the prisoner's wrists with more skill and intelligence than his late brother. Having done this, he backed away and grabbed a blanket in a magician-like fashion. He threw it roughly at the hapless baddie.

Big Nose quickly covered his attractive big cock and was then shunted into a cage. The door slammed with a resounding clang. The newly-instated sheriff took a large ring of keys from the table and secured the bandit behind bars. While Hermie disposed of Hymie, Big Nose sat down on the hard wooden cot, only to leap up again as his bum blisters burst like trodden grapes.

'Well,' said the sheriff, 'tell me just how No-Voice got you.'

Big Nose turned scarlet. Once more his blood got the better of him and crept up in an enormous mound at the head of his horny cock. He muttered furiously to himself.

'Whadyasay?' said Herm.

'You ain't gonna believe me, sheriff.'

'Try me,' said Mr. Rosen (who had lost his Berg too).

'I was camping . . .'

'Oooh ducky,' interjected Herm.

'. . . in a clearing,' continued Joe somewhat snappily. '. . . just off the trail leading to the Superstition Mountains. I'd had my chow and was sitting by the embers of the fire enjoying a final puff . . .'

'. . . Here we go again,' broke in Herm.

'. . . when I heard a rustling . . .'

'. . . Oh, tell me more,' said Herm. 'Rustlers are just what I want to catch . . .'

'. . . in a sagebush behind me. I whipped around, gun in hand and I nearly let off . . .'

'. . . How rude!' shrieked Herm, hysterically.

'. . . a spray of bullets for good measure, when right out of the needlegrass and balsamroot stepped a shimmering vision of shagginess. I shook my head, thinking I was seeing things. But she started toward me. This gal. Never seen anything so raunchy in my life. A great mop of black shiny curls were piled high on her head. Huge round burning eyes and the sweetest bow of a mouth you've ever seen. Her skin was a glowing pinky colour. A black velvet band encircled her lily-white throat. Her shirt was cut low at the front, revealing two finely-contoured hillocks. Below the frills of her blouse, her waist was nipped in by the dark blue band of her skirt. The heavy material was moulded to the shape of her well-rounded hips, then fell away to the ground.'

Big Nose Joe paused in his sexual verbals and licked his lips.

'Go on,' said the panting Herm impatiently. 'What's this got to do with your ensnarement?'

Joe started off again: 'It was her scent. Overpowering it was. Like orange blossoms. She walked, hips undulating towards me. I'd been out on the trail for weeks and I hadn't sniffed a pussy all that time. I dropped my gun as she sashayed towards me. I just kept looking. Sniffing and looking. She smelt powerful good. I was hypnotised by the sight and smell of her. She rattlesnaked right past me and laid down on my bedroll by the fire. The glow of the fire danced on her silken countenance. Her eyes were very bright and full of longing. I stood transfixed – not knowing what to do . . .'

'Oh Gawd . . .' said Herm critically.

'She stared so, first at my face and then at my . . . er . . .' Joe did his colour change act again. 'She stared at . . . er . . .' Joe went even redder. 'Well, after a few minutes, I could feel things heaving up in me chaps. My batwings were on fire and my jinglebobs danced a merry tune. Then she put her finger to her lips and licked it with her moist sensuous tongue. Slowly, she slipped her forefinger into her mouth, which made sharp sucking noises as it went. When her finger reappeared, it was wet and shiny. She lapped at its pointed tip, running it around and around her lips. Suddenly it disappeared, up to the last joint. She moaned softly. I got more and more fidgety and uneasy. She was tugging at her skirt now with the other hand. Yanking it upwards, in the most unladylike manner, she displayed the frothy white lace of her petticoat. Her ankles were very slender. Her tiny feet were encased in short buttoned boots. Fine stockings complimented her long shapely legs. All her thighs were now on show. Above her stocking tops, I could see that wanton strip of peachy skin. She flung her legs wide. Taking her wet finger from her mouth, she ran it down the deep vee between her breasts, then both hands were upon her legs, fingers crawling slowly up the inside of her thighs. She said my name and I nearly jumped out of my skin. She beckoned for me to come closer and then her hand returned to her warm flesh. The hairs on the back of my neck were standing up. I couldn't believe my luck. Things like this didn't happen to Big Nose. My mouth had gone as dry as the grit in the Gobi. My hands which had touched nothing more exciting than the leather of horse-reins in weeks, itched to paw those succulent twin domes. The material covering them was stretched to bursting point. As she squirmed on the ground, one large acorn-shaped nipple escaped from its confines with a loud plop. That was it, I had to get my teeth into something, and here was an offering. I stumbled over to her, as the flickering fire cast shadows on her face. Her hair had come undone and tumbled provocatively onto her bare shoulders. I went down on my knees. Somewhere a lone wolf howled but my senses were deaf to everything other than the hot inviting flesh below me. I was so nearly there. My trembling lips hovered above the proffered nugget. I was an inch from the stiffening baubel. At this proximity, her flowery perfume enveloped me like a cloud. I was a magnet, she the pulling metal. After beans and hash, the taste of her nipple was like honey on my tongue. I could feel the heat rising in waves from her body. As I sucked the life-giving blood, her arm went around my neck. She pushed my hat off and with firm fingers started massaging my stiff and aching muscles. By now it wasn't only my neck that was stiff. My . . . ahem . . . cock was very angry.'

Joe's face was livid, his forehead perspired like Niagara Falls, as he remembered his moment of lust. Sheriff Hermie Rosen was agog. He'd never heard such a tale from one of his jailbirds. Big Nose took a deep breath and once more took up his saga.

'I pushed my hands into the front of her blouse and lifted her breasts free of their muslin trap. The great silky globes spilt over my open palms. I grasped them, squeezing them hard. She gave a sharp intake of breath and sat up. I lost my grip. Her luscious melons danced in front of my face. She put both her arms around the back of my head and pulled herself upwards. Her breasts squashed against the rough fabric of my shirt. With eager hands, I reached up and tore at my buttons. Within seconds, her bare skin was crushed against mine. The cool of her cheek rested against the stubble of my chin. Her hair wound itself around me, ensnaring me in a skein of silk. This was one trap in which I didn't mind being caught. She stuck out her tongue and, with feline grace, slowly licked all over my face. I closed my eyes, giving myself up to this amazing new experience. The only thing I'd ever been licked by before was the odd friendly dog. Gee, this was different. Lovely lappings – over my eyebrows, around my eyes and down my big nose. She laughed softly to herself as she licked the bridge of it. Her hands flashed down to my cock. A tinkling laugh rang out, as her hands closed around it.

"Cockadoodledoo," she whispered, with her tongue in my ear. "Who's a big boy, then?" "I am, I am," I croaked. "Show me," she cried. I leapt to my feet, threw my gunbelt to the ground and foolishly kicked off my boots and trousers. I still had on my cumbersome underwear, but with deft fingers she peeled off my drawers. She exclaimed with delight at the sight of my cock, which stuck out like a flagpole from beneath my shirt. Even I was frightened by the size of it. Oh, I'd had it up a good few times before but never had it seen anything so tasty. "Excuse me, ma'am," I ventured, "where would you like it?" Her eyes widened in horror. "My goodness me," she ventured, "don't you know where that big stick belongs, cowboy? Do I have to show you?"

Without waiting for an answer, she showed me alright. She

sprawled flat on the ground and spread her skirts. I'm not used to all the finery that well-to- ladies have about their person, but I'm sure they wear more than that filly. She had on plenty of petticoats and frilly garters to keep up her stockings, but above them, nothing. She lay there, legs a-dangling. I stood stunned by her bared pussy cheeks. She drew her knees up and pointed with her finger to her thick patch of fair hair. I don't know a great deal about that sort of hair but I'd always imagined that if the tresses on a woman's head were black, then it would be the same down below. But I didn't dwell long on that subject, for beneath the bush was a glittering split jewel. I was drawn like a magpie to the sparkling gem. My cock became a water diviner and between her thighs it'd found a gushing well. She took a firm grip on me and steered me on a straight course. I jumped at her touch. Her hands were on fire. I bent over her and she straightened, so I could slip between. I knelt in the valley of her thighs. Her eyes burnt with a fierce passion. My tip came to rest on her open prairie. Lust overcame me. I stabbed at her bruising the petals of her flower. At the same time, my hand snatched at her blouse. The noise of the fabric ripping to ribbons was deafening but she scarcely seemed to notice or care. She thrust her hips forward and sucked me down her thirsty tunnel of desire. I buried my face in her hair as my cock doodle-dooed. I hardly moved. With uncontrolled gyrations, she screwed herself onto my rod. She moved her tight buttocks around and around. I put my hands underneath the chubby cheeks and pulled her closer. She cried out. Her whole body shuddered. Then spasm after spasm took hold of her. Seeing her open lust like this was the final straw for my stalk. I gave one massive spurt. It would have torn most women in two. But not this one. She let out a yell of pure joy as my month's loneliness culminated and exploded inside her. She clung to me and rode out the storm. Sharp teeth tore into my shoulder. I could feel a trickle of blood running down my arm. The next thing I knew, she had rolled me over and was pinning me to the floor. Although she was no heavyweight, she was as strong as an ox. Her hair covered my face and blinded me. I felt á sharp . . .'

Big Nose broke off in mid stanza. Sheriff Hermie Rosen was not the most sensitive of men and his sense of smell wasn't all it should have been. The heavy aroma of orange blossom had filled the jail. He was totally engrossed in Joe's story; otherwise he might have heard the door open and seen a slim dark girl enter. The menacing shiny-barrelled gun looked far too heavy for so fragile a wrist. But the woman gripped the piece firmly. Big Nose hesitated, unsure whether it would be to his advantage to warn the sheriff of the danger. Too late. The butt of the gun cracked down on the sheriff's skull. It sounded quite hollow – which didn't surprise Big Nose at all . . . while Hermie Rosen lay in the lad of Nod, female garments were thrust through the bars at Joe.

'Come on,' the girl hissed.' 'Put these on.'

Big Nose looked down the barrel of the gun. He dressed in haste, trying to sort out which bit of feminine apparel went where. Alarmed at this transvestite turn, Joe nevertheless realised that his face in the shade of the large black-brimmed bonnet might just pass for that of a horsey woman. Keys jangled in the lock. The heavy door swung open and Big Nose stepped out into semi-freedom. Half relieved and half frightened by this amazing turn of events, Big Nose wondered what his fireside fuck was going to put him through this time. He didn't wonder too long. She pressed the gun up against his breastbone and the cold metal bit into his adam's rib. Together they stepped lightly out of the jail. The bright fierce heat of the day hit them between their four eyes. Few people were out and about, choosing a cool interior in preference to a hot Gold Dust afternoon. A buckboard and pair stood at the ready outside the sheriff's office. The lady helped Big Nose onto the front seat; with a touch of cold steel up his bum! An onlooker would have thought that the younger girl was giving the older more infirm woman, a helping hand. Big Nose was having a fair bit of trouble moving daintily with the voluminous skirt flapping around his shapely ankles. Once he was safely in position, his rescuer got up beside him, took the reins and they trotted off. Not a word was spoken by either until Gold Dust was several miles behind them. Big Nose twisted in his seat then and squinted out from under his bonnet at his captor.

'Whadya want with me?' he enquired. 'You've already had my oats.'

She smiled cheekily. 'Good wasn't it?'

Big Nose was amazed by her lack of modesty. Although, by now, he shouldn't have been surprised by anything this female did.

'She's crazy,' he thought. 'Crazy as Sadie, that gal I knew a long time ago.'

Crazy Sadie suddenly reined in the horses. The buckboard, which had been travelling at great speed, slowed to walking pace. The horses were quite happy at this slow motion. But the prickly fear was upon Big Nose again – and with good reason. A nattily-booted foot shot out and caught him a sharp blow in the balls. This rather unfriendly gesture took Big Nose by surprise. He sailed through the air, his skirts billowing out like a mainsail in a heavy gust of wind. He landed in an ungainly (even for him) heap, hurting nothing more than his manly pride. The breeze grabbed at his skirts. And for the second time that day, Big Nose's bare arse was bathing in the sunlight. Joe scrambled to his feet and looked after the departing wagon. Nothing could be seen, except a huge cloud of dust travelling at breakneck speed towards the high sheer rockface that formed the lower foothills of the Superstition Mountains. Having recently travelled that trail himself, Joe realised that the poor woman was making a grave mistake in heading off towards the mountain range. Nothing lay ahead there, except rough, arid terrain and bloodthirsty Indians. He wasn't unduly worried, though, about the fate of this wanton hussy. His own fate was a matter of much greater importance! He looked around. Desolation; dry buffalo grass as far as the eye could see. He estimated that he must be at least ten miles from Gold Dust.

All he had to protect himself from the still-scorching sun was his bonnet, blouse and skirt. She'd not even left him a canteen of water! And he knew of no $H_2$0-hole between himself and town. He was a cowboy without a horse; as useless as a cock without a cunt. He'd only travelled this trail between the mountains and town once before and then he'd not been looking at the scenery. He knew his chances of hitching a ride on the odd stagecoach were pretty slim. The area was devoid of friendly human life. The choice of travelling companion was limited to Indians, who you couldn't see until they scalped you anyway, or vultures . . . speaking of which . . . He looked up into the clear blue sky and, sure enough, wheeling high overhead were the feathered creatures of death. They had started their slow ominous circle of descent. Joe gathered up his skirts and set off hastily in the direction of Gold Dust. Jail there was better than a bone-picked death out here in the sagebrush. The sharp stones were painful to his sensitive soles and his progress was very slow. Under his breath, he cursed the black-haired abductress. His skirt hampered his steps but he plodded bravely on. The vultures followed, hypnotised by the flesh that would be theirs.

Chapter Two

NO-VOICE DISAPPEARS UP HIS OWN CRACK

Meanwhile, the-Man-With-No-Voice, on leaving Gold Dust with his bounty had headed straight along the trail that lead to the Superstition Mountains. He rode his horse hard, keen to get back to his hideout and start his plans for the next money-making escapade. No one knew the whereabouts of his base. He just seemed to materialise with his prisoners and vanish into thin American air. If someone had been watching the mighty man, they'd have felt sure that he was riding hell-for-leather into a sheer stone cliff-face. But upon gaining the blank wall of stone, he dismounted. It would now have been clear to the onlooker that there were in fact a million cracks in the stone, leading to nowhere – or so it seemed. But No-Voice knew the secret of the black magic hole. He led his mount carefully through a fissure which wound around like a snake. He picked his way through a series of small boulders and eventually came upon a large bush which grew against another dead-end. The hunter pulled the dry branches to one side and led his horse still further, through the minute gap now visible in the wall. On the other side of the hidden opening was a narrow passage. He mounted his horse and trotted down the cleft in the rock. In the shadow of the mountains which towered above, his way was as cold and dark as night. After ten minutes of twisting and turning his steed, the bounty hunter was out of the gloom and, once again, in sunshine. Before him stretched a low flat clearing. On all sides the mountains pressed onto the huntsman's home. There was no way out but the way he'd come in. In the centre of the level hideaway was a small log cabin. To the left of it was a corral, containing a couple of Arabian mounts. The only other sign of life at this bounty hunter's minor ranch was a richly-plumed golden eagle, tethered to a wooden perch on the shack's rickety wooden verandah. As he passed, No-Voice gave the regal bird a friendly fluff of its feathers, and swept on into his inner sanctum. His horse, he left outside.

The interior of the house was bare and functional. In one corner was a humpy bunk. Over the bed hung a horseshoe. A spare gun resting in its holster was suspended from a nearby hook. Two rifles hung on the wall alongside the pit. A pair of woollies, looking like the chopped-off legs of a huge gorilla, were fastened to a post at the bottom of the bed. These winter chaps, he only used when he was Montana-bound. The bedding consisted of a couple of blankets, which were thrown roughly over the hard mattress. Two pairs of boots were slung under the bed. In the opposite corner to the bed was a huge trunk with a rusty lock. An old washbowl stood on a wooden table. Propped up on the table top was a large oval silver mirror. It was a very feminine affair and looked incongruous in these most-masculine of surroundings. No-Voice reached up and pulled at a secret flap high in the wall of his cabin. He raised the small door to reveal a hidden niche. He stuffed his newly-made wad into the cache and closed the flap again. He whipped off his poncho to expose his sensible collarless flannel shirt. He reached into one of the deep pockets and pulled out a key. He walked, with menace in his eyes, across the room. There was more money to be made. And so thinking, and with the key at the ready, he advanced upon the battered old chest . . .

At that moment, Chuck Carson had anything but money on his mind. How they loved and how they laughed. Laughter was always part of their loving. And danger was part of their lives. Rose; her nature was as open and sunny as the flower after which she'd been named. And Chuck. A strong, young brave deputy sheriff. The Carsons had been married two years. Rose taught school.

Chuck knew the brothers Rosen were on the payroll of Jake

Maddon – the smart-suited, smooth-talking businessman who had a smutty little finger in every illegal Gold Dust pie. Chuck had aspirations. And he was a patient man. After all, he'd waited four years to bed Rose. And four years of courting a gal like Rose was a trial for any man! Chuck was used to biding his time. One day, the Rosen brothers would be gone – dead or banished. It ought to be pointed out here that this young dupe had not yet got wind of the demise of Hymie. And Chuck would make sure he was there to put the town to rights. He'd forgotten that only the good die young!

But right now his ambitions were of the orgasmic kind . . . Rose was in his bed – their bed. She looked at her handsome clean-shaven husband. Through the gloom of the heavily-shuttered room, she could just make out his fine outline. Rose loved the smell of him, the touch of his skin, the feel of his taut body, its hard core pressing right into her soft core. They loved to make love in the afternoon. Chuck reached out and took that soft, familiar body into his arms. The rounded shapes of her breasts moved against him, the rigid nuts of her nipples digging deeply into his manly chest. This signal of her need for him drove him ape. It started those stirrings at the back of his balls. He stretched out and traced a finger under her chin; down along the supple skin of her fragile swan's neck. Chuck turned her around and moved in behind her curled naked form. He eased his body around the smooth bend of her bottom. He heard her sigh; a soft contented sound. Rose rolled towards him. Her hands sought him. Her fingers ran long loving lines down his torso. Suddenly her hands dipped and swooped upon his lovestalk. Finding it rising, she grasped the knob tenderly but firmly. Her tremulous passion-paws commenced their task with loving devotion. She pulled, stroked, probed and made him sigh in turn. Tingle; his body tensed and relaxed under her ministrations. She played his instrument a thought it were a Stradivarius. She made him jig to her own sweet melody. Chuck felt her hot breath upon his face. Her tongue raped his mouth. The probe darted in, then out again, then down towards his raging fiery furnace. Fierce, adventurous licks swept over his nipples, bringing them bounding to erection. On she went, over his flat hairless stomach; teasing, tantalising. She travelled down to the smouldering core of masculinity, that she had learnt was her Chuck. Her tongue arrived in the forest of pubic rushes that she knew so well. Her tresses fanned out like sweet-smelling grass. Chuck lay back, inhaling the aroma of her cuntsauce. The scent of her special juices wafted upwards and ravaged his nostrils. He breathed deeply, as though his life depended on the inhalation of her pungent pussy. Her nose, her face and her breasts pressed hard into him. Her tongue flicked in and out of every cranny of his crotch. Around and around the mulberry bush it went. Chuck's patience was running out – just like the sands in the hourglass nearby. Soon he would have to give in to the pulsating demands of his cock. He willed her to stop dallying in the foothills and get to the peak of his Superstitions! As if in silent answer, Rose rose to meet his plea. She licked her lips and salivated her way up the pink shaft. Slowly, and with great love, she bathed him in long loving licks. Up the side of the volcano she crawled, until the two pink lips touched and erupted. Their flames burnt brightly as Chuck positioned himself for the paradise poke. He heaved his lithe frame so that Rose could take his fine spear down her warm deep throat. Rose sucked greedily – a child with its first lollipop – slurping sucking. Such joyous noises floated up to Chuck's ears. He looked down at Rose's face and watched spellbound as his cock flashed in and out of her parted moist lips. Her hands were busy between his cheeks. Fast and furious fingers touched his balls and stroked his thighs. Fingers everywhere; and the tongue still at work, madly licking. The cock shafting. The mouth manipulating. It was too much for him to take any longer. He could not hold back, could not wait. He gave her his all – gallons of his Love Potion Number Ten. She swallowed it to the last drop as the sun shafted across the counterpane. A yellow sunlight beam spilled through the shutters and splashed onto the gold of Rose's fine head. Chuck eyed her contentedly. The light reflected off her hair formed a halo around her head. She looked like the sweet angel she was, as she licked her lips of Chuck's jissome and smiled slowly up at him. Then, his wife came up, all smiling eyes, and joined him on the pillow. Her lips glistened. Her tongue sought his. He closed his eyes and pulled her on top of him. Light as a feather, she lay pressed to him. He slipped his hands under the cheeks of her bottom, around through the dark secret tunnel, until he came upon that lovely warm crack, wet and wanting, waiting for him. Touching it, he felt his sap beginning to rise again. How ever many times he spilt his seed, Rose could always make him puff up with passion once again. She could be so many things – a sunny lady, a quiet lady, a sad lady, a girlish lady. And he loved and fucked all of these women. He pushed her up into a sitting position and her hair tickled his face as it went by. The great golden cloud blew across his sky. Her face floated above him, pink, glowing with love and life. She sat there, full of his spunk. His cock found her bud and slithered in. This was where Chuck wanted to be! His joint gave a jerk for joy. He looked up at her – he loved to see her like this, astride him, her thighs straining, her flat smooth stomach, her tiny waist and above the full creamy orbs of her breasts with their cherry red nipples. And they were all his, all his. With his cock deep inside her rosebud, she looked him straight in the eye and started vibrating her vagina. Hardly had she started on her sexual merry-go-around. Hardly moving. Yet, she still managed to manhandle her spouse's handle with extra-muscular activity. Her eyes held his gaze. She was rocking herself now, upon his fucking stick. He put his hands to her waist and lifted her up a fraction of an inch. She rocked, he lifted, she squeezed. She rocked some more. He lifted some more. She squeezed some more. She sat upon his joystick and felt the bubbling of Chuck on the boil again. She looked at him, full of love and full of passion. Rose rode him for pleasure but most of all for love. Their passions ran away with each other . . . sperm hit the fan.

Chapter Three

VIRGIN ON THE RIDICULOUS

Meanwhile Big Nose Joe was stumbling along with all the elegance of a fettered ostrich in a three-legged race. He was as parched as the landscape that surrounded him. The burning in the back of his throat was like the sun having a climax all of its own in his larynx. His feet were badly cut and bleeding. His problematic corns had long-since been severed from their host. But he still had an air of debonair ruggedness about him! His feathered escorts of death winged around him, not quite as high as they had been minutes before . . . Joe's head was thumping. His mind reeled. The pain was all and his spirit gave way. His knees buckled and he fell into the short, hairy buffalo grass. The dry vegetation scratched his face and arms and stray bits of the tough weed poked up his nostrils. Joe got to all fours but he couldn't make it any higher. So he crawled towards Gold Dust. Well, it was the only way to travel! He'd progressed about two hundred yards in this slow and painful fashion, when he heard the noise of horses hooves in the distance. Big Nose scrambled around to face the oncoming rider.

'Was it an Apache or perhaps a Sauvage?' he thought to himself worriedly.

He rubbed his eyes trying desperately to rid them of dust. Blinking hard, he stared with horror into the haze. Into view came The-Man-With-No-Voice.

'Oh no,' yelled Big Nose aloud.

From somewhere he found the strength to get to his feet. And holding his skirts waist high, he fled as fast as a fettered ostrich could. The lasso whistled through the air, faster than a snake through grass. Over Big Nose's head, the lariat slipped. It came to rest in a neat, tight belt around his waist. He jerked backwards and fell on his arse. No-Voice approached the spectacle. Big Nose in women's clothes was quite a picture. Joe's big nose sniffed. He was sure he'd caught a whiff of Crazy Sadie's perfume. He looked around wildly. 'Where could that woman be hiding?' he thought. The scent vanished. The bounty hunter pointed to the mule tethered to his saddle. Big Nose knew he had no choice but to lay over the beast and be taken quietly and uncomfortably back to Gold Dust and jail. No-Voice led him to the mule, watched as the prisoner obediently slung himself over the donkey's back and then set about securing the helpless Big Nose to the animal. Ropes cut into the prisoner's wrists as the mysterious bounty hunter made sure of his knots. When he was certain Joe was safely aboard, he hitched the skirts of Joe's fetching trousseau and raised the garment over the poor jailbird's head. Once again he exposed Joe's arse to mid-West elements.

Gold Dust was stirring up what little nightlife it could muster, as the bizarre duo hit town. Sheriff Hermie Rosen was nursing a sore head, whilst banging small nails into a poster outside the jail. No-Voice was delighted to see that the reward on Big Nose had doubled. The lawman stood back to admire his handiwork. Turning to face the street, he saw Big Nose with his bonneted head peeping out from his upturned skirt. He split his sides. He sat on the sidewalk, while huge tears of mirth tumbled down his lined face. No-Voice waited patiently for the sheriff to control his hysterics.

They showed no sign of subsiding. The donkey, outraged by this pathetic show of idiocy, lashed out with his two back legs and dealt the unfortunate sheriff a fatal blow to the balls. While the third Rosen brother, Herbie, disposed of the corpse, No-Voice assisted, with an elegant gesture, his bonneted ladyfriend down from her ride of joy. Big Nose would never make a real lady, however. He tripped over his hem, fell on his face, and thought sadly that he had spent most of the last twenty-four hours in some sort of arse-up situation. Things couldn't get worse! The threesome went into the most-recently appointed sheriff's office. Big Nose was put straight into clink, while the lawman, bristling with new efficiency and crying huge tears while he did it, counted out the price on Joe's nose.

'This time you ain't gonna escape, goy,' spat the third sheriff Rosen. 'My poor departed brother was a fool to fall for your pack of lies about the leg-over who leapt out of the bushes. You just made up that darned story, so your partner could sneak up behind him and bushwhack him.'

No-Voice reflected that Rosen III seemed to have more intelligence than Rosens I and II and he'd probably not fall for another yarn, if Big Nose had any more up his chaps. He left the dubious double-act to their own devices and sped off into the technicolour sunset. This wily sheriff had the sense to sit facing the door as he interrogated Big Nose. Joe decided to tell lies this time, because no one, not even another stupid Rosen, would believe the truth.

'How come,' started the sheriff, 'yer all done up in a gal's Sunday frills? You'd never pass for a woman – you're far too ugly with that great conk.' The sheriff chortled to himself. But he would have stopped in mid-chortle, if he had known that, right then, the territorial marshal was heading for town.

A might pretty sight that was too, indeedy y'all!

The Marshal rode upon a fine white horse. Nearing Gold Dust, the top cop came upon a small homestead. The land was not at all fertile around there but the folks just about managed to scrape a living. It was better than dying of tuberculosis back east anyway. Daddy Webster, who owned this pitiful patch of land, had the disease bad. Hearing a horse, Webster and his son Matthew took up their positions on the porch of their tumbledown hovel and levelled their shotguns at the intruder. Ma Webster remained inside – scared shitless. A thin wasted woman with the hardship of her life showing in her face, she remained silent during these few tense moments. Webster's finger started a slow squeeze on the trigger. His eyesight wasn't too good but son Matthew's was.

'Gee, dad,' yelled the boy, 'put up your iron. It's a lady!'

The territorial marshal swung down from her horse and Old Webster's gullet went as dry as a chicken's coop. This gal had as many undulations as the hills back wherever the fuck he came from. The men gaped. The silence was broken by a creaking door. Mrs. Webster had crept snail-like out of her shell. Her tight pursed mouth became even more pinched when she saw the newcomer had tits. And there was no mistaking that. Her straight grey split riding skirt was fringed down both sides. Her gun emphasised her femininity, its naked barrel pointed suggestively at her crotch. Tucked into her skirt was a shirt of red and white check linen. It strained under the pressure of swelling melons and the buttons couldn't stop it gaping at the front. A red kerchief was tied at her open neck. A neat brown leather belt, edged in red, nipped in her waist. The gun holster matched the belt. A red sugarloaf sombrero with heavy grey cord around the base sat upon her head. Wisps of copper-coloured hair escaped the rim of the hat and framed her face with a firebird glow.

'Good evening folks, I'm Clit Westwood.'

The men quivered for they'd heard of this Marshal. Her reputation had spread for miles and grown men trembled, their arseholes puckering up in fright, whenever they knew she was in town. But it was those who lived on the wrong side of the law that had most to fear. This legendary lawlady, they'd heard, could waste a man easier with her steaming snatch and ruby lips than with the fancy-handled shooter, dangling like some steel accessory, at her side. Her captured baddies, she always brought into town limp, shamefaced and tied like hogs across her saddle. The men she brought in were always buttoned up and kept their sorry secret to themselves. They were tight-lipped and tight-arsed about their experiences. One or two loudmouths, however, had blabbed while stewed on Gold Dust hooch – a popular proprietory brand in this neck of the woods. The legend of her conquests by cunt, and by gun, had thus began to grow until it had spread like a prairie bushfire across the West.

As she swung herself down from the mighty steed, Matthew couldn't fail to notice that her cullottes were crotchless. He got a brief glimpse of furry fan. It quite shocked him, because Matthew was a virgin – virgin on the ridiculous. His shorthorn became a longhorn inside the dark interior of his buckskin-fortified trousers.

'Why're you folks packing up?' she enquired pointing to the waggon, which was partially loaded with the family's meagre belongings.

Webster spat on the ground. 'It's that Jake Maddon, ma'am. He's been tryin to make us sell up for years. We've stuck it as long as we can but I think we're licked this time. He's headed off our water and we won't live a week. Our two cows and the plants which we've tended for years, are all dying. Maddon is a bastard. He only wants to buy the land up cheap so he can sell it again for a fortune, when the railroad comes through. This time he's got us beat. If all the other small ranches lose their water, they'll be forced, like us, off the land. There's only me and the boy. We're not strong enough to take on Maddon's gang.'

'You must all stay. I'm going to ride into Gold Dust and sort out that villain Jake once and for all. And his cronies, the Rosen Brothers – I've heard about them too. You just go back inside and I'll tell Matthew my plan.'

Muttering and wheezing consumptively, Webster and his missus went inside. Clit turned the full force of her charm on the youth.

'You've got to persuade your ma and pa to stay, boy. If they run away they'll be on the move forever. This land is their land, this land is your land . . .'

And so trilling, Clit danced with the boy to the barn. Matthew, bewildered, followed where he was lead. Like a steer to the knackers yard. Once inside, his bewilderment gained ground, as Clit threw him roughly into the hay. This brutality made his virginal knob rocket off into the buckskin. Having exploded and let loose the first loveload of his life (nice boys like Matthew didn't masturbate – they were just prone to headaches), he wasn't sure what to do next. The Marshall stood with her legs astride his head and promptly sat on his face. He licked sheepishly at her laid-bare sexgash, but this didn't satisfy her at all. In a second, her fingers were at his flies. His boots flew in all directions, his trousers hit the hay and revealed the sorry mess that had once been bright young pulsating manhood.

'Came in your drawers, did you?' queried Clit.

'Yes,' he stammered.

At this, she unbuttoned her marshall's star and it dropped to the ground with a clank. Her clothes quickly followed and Matthew witnessed the fastest striptease in the west. She lay down beside him on the hay and pushed her bare arse towards him. Their left legs bent together. She squirmed, pressing into the soggy mass of cock and balls. With her cunt in position, Clit kept twitching her clit over his flabbiness. She put her fiery electric socket to his thirteen amp plug. His current came on again immediately, passing her sex voltage to his power point. A hot lick of energy devoured him. She parted her lower lips and manoeuvred his cock between the two velvety pads. They dropped kisses on his broad fat sex slug. Her bottom ground into him. Taking his hand, she guided it through her pubic patch until it came to rest on her bulging well-formed mons. Matthew held the moving mound in his hand, wondering at the peachy softness of the multiple folds. He had no idea there were so many nooks and crannies that went to make up a woman. Her fingers came down to steer his slippery length between the eager lusting lips of her pussy. The head of his cock broached her portals and her mammoth muscles – so experienced – sucked him up with aplomb or all the dexterity of a vacuum cleaner. His fingers stroked excitedly at the tangle of matted hair. In sheer desperation, he held his hand fast againt her sex slot. He hardly had to move because she did the doing. Her breathing seemed almost inhuman to his ears. Nails raked through the hay as great gasps tore from her body. She worked her bottom furiously, like the piston of some sex-sodden machine. Her hand crushed down on his fingers, pushing them firmly against her bulge. With a long loud unearthly moan she came, quivering, pushing, scratching, attacking the straw bed as though contact with it might ease the pleasurable pain that enveloped her. He lay in shock, waiting for her violent spasms to subside. He froze with his rod erect and encased in the warm heart of her cunt. She was sighing gently now. His hand was still paralysed, glued to her man-trap.

'It's your turn,' she gasped, and his instinctive sex urge took over.

He turned her suddenly, squashing her face into the straw pillow. Her arms splayed out. He pulled out his trapped and juiced-up hand and clasped her on either side of her hips. He wrenched backwards and her bottom bounced upwards. His prick prodded her soft pudding. He looked down at the dark valley between the lovely pale moons of her bum. Matthew was in awe at this unexpected new sensation. The feel of Clit's never-ending tunnel, so tight yet so yielding, was beyond his wildest virgin dreams. She turned her head and he gazed at her delicate profile. The shades of moonlight coming through the holed roof of the shippen dallied on her fresh complexion. Her fists clenched. Her eyes closed tight. She waited for the next onslaught of his masculine ardour. He backed off a little, mesmerised, as a couple of his thick inches fell out of the secret hole. His moment had come again. He felt Clit brace herself and he slammed home hard. She almost disappeared into the hay beneath the force of the blow. He pulled her back roughly and banged her rotten. Reaching around and under, she fingered herself and then went for his balls. He stopped his powerful pumping, as she scored his tightening bollock-sack. She weighed them in her hands, as her insides closed in on his thumping phallus, milking his creamy come from the very roots of his balls.

Post-coital whisperings were drowned out by the sound of a combine harvester.

Matthew found himself totally convinced of the need to stay. Buttoning up his trousers, he strode into the house to try and persuade his father.

Clit roared off into the night intent on cleaning up Gold Dust once and for all.

At this very moment, Chuck (Goody Goody) Carson was on his way to the Websters. Jake Maddon's action in cutting off the water supply from the homesteaders around the town had quickly become old news in Gold Dust. Chuck, still forgetting that the good die young, was prepared, at last, to make a stand against the evil Maddon. He had already, with his sincerity and good looks, persuaded the others to put up a fight and he was now approaching the shadowy shape of the Webster's hovel, unaware that they'd already been coverted to the ways of the cunt. He discovered Matthew, shagged to death, lying on the verandah, while ma and pa unloaded their pitiful possessions from the waggon. With great perspicacity Chuck said: 'I see you folks are staying after all.'

'Tis the boy,' said Father Webster. 'He's been persuaded by the famous Marshall Clit Westwood. She's on her way to town now to call a meeting against the Maddon gang.'

Chuck didn't bother to question the family further. He rode off in considerable haste, anxious to meet the great and good law person. He rode hard into the blackness. He was just slowing down to navigate a narrow pass, which was a short-cut into town, when he felt sure he smelt a strong sweet cloying scent. It reminded him of orange blossom – but it surely couldn't be that, out here in this barren wasteland. There was nothing around for miles except cottonwoods and hackberries.

Thwack.

Something fell out of a tree, knocked him from his horse

and the black still night enveloped him, as he gave way to unconsciousness.

Clit tied her horse to the rail and kicked open the door to Rosen's office. He wasn't there. She crossed the wide main street to the telegraph office, intent on sending a message along the wires back to her headquarters. She burst in on a hold-up. Who should be holding up the joint but the sheriff himself.

'What the hell d'you think your doing?' she barked at the wayward Herbie.

Telegraph operator Tibbs waved his arms in the air and babbled incoherently. He calmed down considerably when he saw the huge glittering star, strategically placed on one of Clit's tits. He threw himself into a huge grovel and with eyeshade askew, the wee hole below his pencil-line moustache fell open.

'That darn, no-good sheriff is tinkering with me equipment.'

Rosen levelled his gun at the new arrival. Tibb's verbal diarrhoea showed no sign of abating. He continued to spill the beans. But Rosen showed no signs of giving in either. His finger pressure increased on the gun's trigger.

'He's trying to cut the wires so that you can't send your customary message of arrival back to HQ.'

'So that was his little game,' thought Clit.

If her message didn't get back, her superiors would think that she'd been bushwhacked on the trail and that's what Maddon and the Rosens wanted them to think. They, meanwhile would have cut her up and disposed of the body. She thought quickly and moved even faster. Her leg shot up in the air in the direction of Rosen's piece but her boot didn't even make contact with metal. It was the sight of her pussy that was his undoing. It was years since he'd seen one and the shock killed him outright. His agonising cries brought the last of the Rosen quads to the rescue. While Hilton Rosen disposed of Herbie's body, Clit sent her message. Taking over as only a woman with stars on her tits could, Clit frogmarched the unfortunate Jewish sheriff back to his own jail. She bundled him into the building and told him to stay there and stay out of trouble. And keep a big eye on Big Nose too.

Knowing she had to make the first move to bring Jake Maddon out into the open, Clit sashayed down the sidewalk towards Lurex's saloon. Jollification noises reached her ears. A lot was happening in Tex's fun palace. Music, laughter and the clinking of glasses. Composing herself for action, Clit stood outside the double swing doors. With hand at the ready near her gun, she took a deep breath and burst into the brightly-lit room, bouncing the doors off her bosom as she went. Her tits arrived in the room half a second before she did. A hush descended. Eyeballs bulged from sockets. Mouths gaped. And the floozies looked flummoxed.

'I'm the Territorial Marshall,' she exclaimed to the stupefied crowd. 'I know what Jake Maddon's up to and I'm going to put a stop to it right now.'

At the mention of the name Maddon, a crack formed in the crowd. Several cowpokes stepped swiftly back to reveal the man himself. He was at the poker table with Lurex Tex, who was draped like a brightly-plumed parrot on his shoulder. This indecent exposure caused a ripple of excitement to run through the crowd of cows and their pokes!

Maddon rose from his seat, knocking the poker table flying. Tex almost went with it but in the nick of time grabbed a thigh for support. With an elegant flick of his leg, he freed himself of this womanly impediment and walked slowly towards the bristling Clit Westwood.

'Well, shag me short, if it isn't the famous lady Marshall.'

A semi-circle of thugs moved up behind their bossman. Meanwhile, the other inhabitants of Gold Dust were attempting to crawl into the woodwork, proving, once and for all, the worms that they were. Clit, not at all intimidated, could only think that the boys were intent on a gangbang. 'How jolly,' she thought. But there was no time for that at the moment – she had other things on her mind. Ignoring the thickset pinstriped man in front of her, she addressed the worms in the wood.

'Ain't none of you boys gonna help here?' she enquired blazing.

'But we'll get ourselves killed,' ventured one bright spark at the back.

'That don't matter – we've been dead for years,' said another.

Maddon and Clit's eyes met as they puffed up like a couple of cocks about to peck the living daylights out of each other. They'd both opened their mouths and drawn breath about to speak, when their confrontation was rudely interrupted by a vision of ripped loveliness which fell through the swing doors and onto the wooden floor of the saloon. A grubby, blood-stained hand reached out in a begging gesture of helplessness. A blond matted head painfully lifted itself from the floor only to fall, bonk, back down again. Chuck Carson looked as though he'd been savaged by Indians – even though his scalp was still intact.

Big-hearted Bossyboots Westwood momentarily forgot her mission in her concern for the young and lovely man in distress. She turned on a spiked heel and bent to assist the unconscious Chuck. Jake was presented with grey-clothed buttocks and very little else. Upset by this flanelette rebuff, he returned to his poker. His henchmen righted the table and he took his place behind it while ordering Tex to return to her perch. Clit rolled back Chuck's foreskin and decided that there was nothing for him but open-cock surgery. Doc Halliday lived only two wooden shacks away, and it didn't take the strong lass long to hump him down to the surgery.

The Doc, unaware that people were approaching, was at that second parking his hands squarely over Rose Carson's best friend's cunt. It was all but steaming under the patch of her corn-coloured pubes. Her eyes were wide and innocent, as she lay back on the examination couch allowing the elderly doctor an uninterrupted passage to her dripping jewel. He clenched his cheroot firmly between his teeth and concentrated on maintaining as professional an air as he could muster, under the unusual circumstances. It was a long time since he'd had such a pretty chicken come to him for medication and a happy change from prodding the fat guts of the whisky-swilling soaks who made up ninety per cent of his patients.

'She ain't no virgin, but by Jesus, she's lovely,' mused the good doctor to himself.

He stuck a finger firmly into her gluey crack and whirled it around with abandon. He then withdrew the pretend phallus and examined the wetness upon its length. The girl's cunt muscles sighed and contracted with a tiny plop. She blushed at the sound and caught the doctor's eye. He fixed her with what he hoped was a fatherly look and said:

'Now, if you'll just turn over, my dear.'

Sweating, he mopped his brow quickly, as she rearranged herself face-down on the bed. He placed his listening device – or was it his ear – on her back, eyeing her deliciously rounded bum as he did so. He walked stiffly around the foot of the bed, stooping to squint up her arse. The girl made no complaint whatsoever as he parted her legs, massaging her calves gently and commenting on the healthy tone of her thighs. He enquired in an off-hand manner as to whether she had suffered recently from the vapours or from any foreign blemishes of the private parts, whether she was regular and, polishing his glasses furiously, whether she felt forced at any time to rub herself between her legs to relieve the tension she felt from teaching school with Rose.

Her head turned away. The girl answered quietly in the affirmative to the last question asked. Whereupon the doctor enquired whether she would be good enough to demonstrate to him the exact method she employed. Still not looking at him, the girl moved onto her side, brought her fingers to her mouth to moisten them, stretched her legs together and placed the three middle fingers on her crack. Then, breathing deep and long and thrusting her head well back, she pointed her toes and frigged herself briskly.

Doc Halliday brought his head close to where the action was, sniffing the musky perfume of her snatch. With impeccable bedside manners, he refrained from touching and fished, instead, for his bursting member beneath the bed. The girl was panting now, her fingers slipping in and out of her moistened slot. Her nipples stood out like two pink antennae. She was in a world of her own and it was then the Doc entered his. Clambouring between her now parted, thrashing legs, he aligned his gnarled and knotted instrument with her orifice and mouthing vain Hippocratic oaths, plunged it unceremoniously in.

Clit fell in through the front door with Chuck over her shoulder, to find the doc having his quick incision. The patient he'd been interfering with fled the wooden examining couch on their arrival. Halliday swiftly wiped his dick on a surgical swab, tucked it behind his rubber apron and took a quick swig from his half-empty liquor bottle. He wiped the back of his hand hygienically over his nose and said, 'I thought it was blood but it's not!'

'We have a patient here for you, Doc,' said Clit.

'Why it's Chuck Carson,' he replied through the slurs. 'Doggone, what a mess. Looks like he's been railroaded by an iron horse.'

Peeved at the medicine man's lack of concern, Clit fetched him a blow to the head, which had a distinctly sobering effect.

He made a quick and efficient examination and pronounced that rigor mortis had set in.

'Surely that's only an erection, doctor,' said Clit, stroking her Matthew-passion-saturated inner thigh.

'Your perspicacity astounds me,' burbled the alcoholic medic.

And he continued his investigations and found that Chuck was suffering from an acute case of concussion.

'Hmmm,' said the doctor. He prodded a neat set of eight

scratches with his gnarled little fingers, which were emblazoned on the deputy's shoulders and inner thighs.

'Looks like he's been savaged by a wild grizzly while he was bare!'

'But there are no bears, grizzly or otherwise in this vicinity,' cried the quizzical Clit.

As she spake, Chuck's adequate sternum stirred.

'I think he's on the mend,' said the knowledgeable doctor.

The dry, cracked lips opened.

'Rape. I was raped,' croaked Chuck.

'Tch. Tch. Tch.,' wailed the doctor. 'Bestiality yet again rears its ugly head in Gold Dust.'

At the mention of rape, the local newshound, who'd been sniffing at the keyhole, fell agog through the door. This was the biggest scoop he'd had in years.

Scribbler Ferret looked like the animal after which he'd been named. The Marshall gave an imperious wave of her hand and he backed into the corner and sat upon a commode, pencil poised.

'Who did you rape?' questioned Clit.

'I have been debauched,' groaned Chuck. 'Up-ended and taken advantage of. I was just minding my own business riding Trigger back to Gold Dust, when, blow me, if someone didn't say "Blow me". As I was staring down the barrel of a shotgun at the time, I couldn't refuse.'

Clit scrutinised Chuck in disbelief.

Undaunted, Chuck continued his sorry saga. 'I was stiff with fear and frightened rigid and my cock had risen to the occasion.'

The Marshall gave him a prod in the privates. 'Why should anyone rape you? Do you think you're so attractive? Did she tear your clothes off?'

'No, I took my clothes off – but under considerable duress.'

'Did you holler for help?' came the inquisitor.

'I'm a deputy, I don't know how to holler.'

'Why did she need a gun? If I made up my mind that I wanted you, I wouldn't need a gun.'

'She took me by surprise and the short and curlies. Something that felt like tits blotted out the prairie moon. And then she was upon me. And the ravishing commenced. She took my virtue ruthlessly. Without love. Without tenderness. Even without any foreplay. She just sucked my cock rudely into her body. She whispered no sweet nothings in my ear. She had her wicked way with me and left me for dead in the dust.'

Scribbler's lead snapped and he sank into the commode. He went into a daze. His very first scoop. He could see the headlines now: *Deputy Raped By Mystery Lady Falling From Tree*. That would sell at least thirty seven copies. Scribbler had great difficulty extricating his arse from the hollow commode. With a rude plop he was gone to catch the first editions.

As the door banged shut after Scribbler, it opened immediately to a wide-eyed, tear-stained, white-faced Rose – her petals all of a droop. Taking in the scenario in the doctor's surgery, Rose's optics flashed from her husband's frighteningly big dick to Clit's heaving great mammaries. For someone like Rose who taught school, it was all too much. She fainted clean away. Luckily the doctor was still nearby and as he slipped his hand into her bodice to feel for her heartbeat, she came to. Discovering the doctor's hand was still down and Chuck's cock was still up, she was overcome with shame at this apparent orgy. When her husband's disgrace was explained to her by the unbelieving Clit, poor Rose became even more agitated. She burst prettily into tears at the thought that threats could inspire her husband to such weak-willed williness. And the leak of lust on Clit's boots did nothing to allay her fears.

Chapter Four

BRIEF ENCOUNTER WITH A ROPE

Meanwhile, Big Joe was hung – well hung . . .

Chapter Five

BILL AND BEN . . . DEFLOWERED MEN

Meanwhile, back at the saddlers, Old Bill Kennett lived with his brother Ben. In an old wooden shack a mile from Gold Dust where the road ran down into Deadman's Gulch, the two brothers had their domicile and a still at the back. They lived on a lot of rye and very little water! When Bill was sober, he was the best saddlemaker for fifty miles around. But these days he didn't sew many saddles. One morning he was sitting with his brother, Ben, nursing a splitting headache, when the door was kicked in. A slim figure in a poncho stood in the opening, idly smoking a long narrow weed. There was a moment's silence, then old Bill turned to old Ben and said, 'I guess we have a visitor.'

'I guess so,' came the reply.

The-Man-With-No-Voice (but a long weed) indicated that they both should follow him outside. There, the hunter wrote in the sand: 'SADDLE QUICKLY.' and whipped a crumpled piece of paper from deep in the heart of his poncho. Drawn, in a No-Voice fashion, was the saddle that he required.

'Is that so,' said old Bill.

No-Voice nodded.

Bill paused. This customer was unusual and had an air of calm, collected ruthlessness about him. The old stager knew from experience that this visitor spelt danger, yet his hang-over made him testy. He thought, 'I'll rile this No-Voice.'

'Look boy,' he said disdainfully. 'I make saddles for men, not boys with smooth skins and fancy gloves.'

He raised a glass of rye to his lips. Something as black as and as swift as a jet-propelled raven in flight zoomed in front of his eyes. There was an ear-splitting sound of shattering glass. When the noise died away, old Bill found himself with an empty hand. A trickle of rye ran through his fingers. The glass lay in a thousand fragments in the dust.

'Don't you cross me,' said No-Voice's eyes.

Ben, who was smoking his clay pipe at the time, moved forward in protest. He was left with a bowl in his hand as the stem skimmed through the air and out of sight.

No-Voice was instantly back scribbling in the sand. In a few swift strokes, he had drawn a diagram of the extraordinary looking saddle. Attached to the top of the seat was a long roping horn and the unusual thing about this heavy-handed ramming tool or pommel was that it was inclined towards the rider rather than away.

Bill pointed a stubby finger at the instrument. 'What is that?' he enquired.

Like a magician, No-Voice drew his trump-card from up his poncho. In his hand was a ten-inch phallic object, with a gold ring on its base. With the other hand, he palmed off a roll of dollar bills. The stick again flew across the sand, leaving the words 'IN ONE MONTH,' etched in the dust. No-Voice whirled upon his elegant heels, mounted his horse and cantered off over the horizon.

Old Bill sat silently for a moment. Then two gnarled hands stretched out and counted the money lying there.

'Hmpf, he pays well. I guess I'll make this crazy saddle.'

He reached out for his rye bottle which stood precariously on a barrel. A glass was a waste of time anyway. He took a few swigs of the fire water straight down. Then he took the money roll inside the shack and slipped it under a loose board.

Rose was distraught. Chuck had taken her home but had been unable to calm the hysteria mounting in her breast. Chuck found himself standing in a pile of shattered Sunday-best crocks. The furious filly had hurled every piece of china at her seemingly wandering stud of a husband. There was nothing Chuck could do to calm her. He made to unbutton his fly and she fled from the house and hot-footed to her best friend, Millie.

Millie, still recovering from Doc Halliday's ministrations, was sitting with her bum in a bath of hot water. Nevertheless, she welcomed her fraught friend and listened open-mouthed to Rose's tale of woe-ho-ho.

Three days later, having avoided all Chuck's attempts to contact her by fair means and foul, Rose had gone off the rails. Determined to get her own back on the bastard, she had decided to enrol with Lurex Tex at the fun parlour. She had quickly come to this decision, spurred on by the scurrilous newspaper stories that had taken up the whole front page of the local rag. When Rose had been out on the street, going to and from school, people had whispered and nudged and pointed. She couldn't face her school children any longer. They had been ruthless in their taunting.

Lurex Tex was surprised and pleased by this new addition to her fading troupe of belles. Tex invited the naive schoolmarm to her plush downstairs salon. Tex took off Rose's glasses and freed her hair from the prim little bun that Rose wore at the nape of her neck.

'Take off these fuddy-duddy clothes,' Tex told teacher.

As the frumpish raiments fell self-consciously to the floor, Tex felt a strange excitement radiating throughout her body. As she watched Rose taking off her last piece of clothing, it grew even stronger. This odd tremour came unmistakenly from her pubis. The shock of this discovery, after fifteen years or more of unimaginable sexual variety with men, left her faint and breathless. Rose was such an unusual fresh recruit to the Lurex stable – pure, white and a one-cock woman. Tex had no doubt in her mind about her preference. She had been raised on a steady diet of good hard cock and nothing would change her liking for it. Just because she now found herself in the throes of some novel diversion, this didn't mean that she had taken the slow boat to Lesbos. Rose stood naked for her inspection. Tex would always carefully inspect her newcomers. Rose pirouetted shyly for the madame, showing first her breasts and then her bum. Tex reached under the bed and brought out a dildo, hygenically wrapped in a clean piece of linen. Up to now she'd only used it on herself. She trembled in awesome anticipation as she thought about what she'd do to Rose. Rose, after all, was in an unhappy frame of mind at the moment and any relief could only do the gal good. The tool was long and curved, with a large black bulbous head shaped just like a phallus. Rose's hand flew to her mouth to supress her surprise. Tex handed the tremulous maiden a slug of neat whisky.

'Sip this,' she barked.

Rose, suddenly needing Dutch courage and caps to proceed with her revenge on her husband, downed the liquor in one. It went straight to her knees and she started giggling in a somewhat brazen fashion. She advanced on the bed, climbed in beside Tex and then, giggling some more, turned her delicious rump to the older girl.

Tex licked the head of the rubber prick and kneeling between Rose's legs, inserted the tip carefully into the girl's tiny pink purse. She pushed it further in and watched the petals unfold, the orifice widen. Rose squealed with delight and curved her back to push hard against the negroid intruder. It was all inside her now, with just the handle protruding from between her thighs. Rose dropped her head and looked between her legs at the strange object. Beyond, Tex's parted lips accentuated her concentrated expression.

'Fuck me with it,' Rose begged.

Tex plunged the phallus in and out of the gasping girl. Its wet slurping sounds filled the room. That and Rose's sharp cries. It presented a strange spectacle – this scene on the bed. Hilton Rosen thought he must be dreaming. Being far more knowledgeable on sexual matters than his three late brothers, he's heard about these people but had never expected to see such a scene before his very eyes. Not In Gold Dust anyway. One girl had her face buried in the bed and her bum in the air, while the other knelt behind her. A gleaming black object was appearing and disappearing between the first girl's thighs. Hilton stood rivetted to his rowlocks, his eyes stuck to a crack in the shutters. His heart hammered so loud in his chest that he felt sure the occupants of the room would hear him. He strained on tiptoe shaking from his head to his toes to get a better view. By now, Tex had withdrawn the phallic object. She straddled the younger girl's face. Rose was on her back beneath the big quim. And as Hilton's eyes bulged like frog's peepers out of his leathery head, she lowered her head between Rose's legs and slowly brought her mouth into contact with the girl's pink-petalled cunt. Marshall Clit Westwood came around the corner just then and stopped dead in her tracks, as she saw Sheriff Rosen, his face flattened to the boards, ejaculate from between his fingers and right into his fine Stetson. Clit quickly stepped back into the shadows, lifted her skirts and masturbated into her boots. Behind her came Chuck, snorting and frigging like a locomotive. He had seen Clit's climax, and was feeling so frustrated now that Rose had gone, that he just had to bring it out and let it rip. Little did he know that this sexual chain-gang started with Rose getting her rocks off . . . with a woman.

A month later, the door to old Bill and old Ben's shack flew open. But this time, to the men's amazement, a beautiful young girl stood looking down at them. She wore a cornflower blue dress of fine silk, buttoned from the waist up to the neck. Fragrant orange blossom filled the air. A large straw hat with a blue ribbon sat upon her cascading chestnut hair. Such a sight was a rarity in Deadman's Gulch and the two old soaks stared dumbfounded into her eyes. She spoke in a soft musical voice:

'My brother called a month by and ordered a saddle. He's asked me to call and collect it for him. He said to prove I am his sister that I should give you these.'

She held out a bottle of rye and a long clay pipe. The bemused old men watched in silence as she put the gifts down. She walked over to the dummy horse that stood in the corner, on which the resplendant new phallic saddle sat. She fingered the pole. With a thoughtful smile, she expertly examined the leather piece and then turned to the old men and cooed:

'I guess you've done a mighty fine job. I'm grateful and to prove it I'm going to thank you in my own way. Which of you is coming first?' she added, unbuttoning her blouse and walking between them into the back bedroom.

The old men looked at each other as if they'd been struck by lightning and remained immobile until the bell-like voice called again:

'Come on Bill and Ben, don't stand there like flower pot men. I haven't got all day you know.'

As if in a trance, old Bill got up and walked to the door. He almost fell over in deep shock, when he saw the exotic stranger stepping naked out of her dress. She walked towards him and, taking him by the hand, slammed the door. Every sort of emotion flittered through old Bill's mind. He took full stock of her upstanding tits and spreading fair bush, which started in soft down just below her navel. With a quick motion, she pushed him on the bunk, hoiked up his legs and pulled off his boots. With expert hands, she ripped off his breeches and shirt. Then, she stood back put her fingers to her lips and looked at the naked old body covered in tousled grey hair. Old Bill, embarrassed, put his hands over his cock and balls, which were, all three, shrunken by hundreds of bottles of rye. With a firm gesture, No-Voice's sis pulled his hands away and, getting on her knees, took his balls in her right hand and his cock in her red mouth. The old man gave a great shriek of mingled fear, amazement and pleasure, as she started to manipulate and suck. At first his dong remained limp and small. Stopping for a moment, she told him to shut his eyes, then she moved her legs over his body and brought her great hairy hedgehog down on his face, wiping her wet clit backwards and forwards over him. Suddenly, old Bill forgot the years he'd been pickling in rye. Once again he was a young man – six foot tall with a lithe figure and riding into Gold Dust, with his kid brother Ben by his side, travelling up to Lurex Tex's mum's bar, the Buffalo. Belle would take him by the hand and lead him into the woodhouse behind the kitchen and lie with him until dawn. As the fair publes stroked his face, he remembered Belle's bush. She'd had dark hair and behind it a lovely soft cunt. As quickly as it had come, the growth removed itself from his face and a pair of smooth hands gently placed his erect cock upright into her luscious wet hole. He was a youth fucking Belle again in the woodshed. With a great heave and yell he came for the first time in fifteen years and passed out with the sheer pleasure of it all.

Quietly leaving him in the Land of Belle, she walked back into the outer room. Ben was sitting smoking his clay pipe as if nothing had happened. She flung a horse blanket on the floor and pulled the mesmerised old man down beside her. It took a little longer to undress Ben, as one of his boots got stuck and she had to stand up and pull hard, pushing with her other leg on his crotch, before she could remove the thing. When he was totally undressed, one look told her she had a problem. She knew that to leave a cock undunked makes it shrink. He obviously hadn't used his cock, except to pee, for twenty odd years. She could hardly see it. Somehow, though, she managed to give it a slow blow. Unfortunately it got smaller still, seeming to dissolve at the touch of her tongue. Puzzled, she took her mouth away. Then, as if relieved, he stretched out and took his pipe from the table. Striking a match, he leaned back and puffed away like billyo. It was a mortal insult. All her womanly pride was revolting against his indifference. She determined to see that whatever happened, he came. But how? Thoughtfully, she regarded him as he contentedly puffed away. At last, a plan came into her head and a smile flickered across her lips. She leaned forward and took his pipe out of his mouth and inserted its long stem up her orange-blossom-scented cunt. She pushed the clay dildo until it reached the entrance of her womb. She squeezed her legs hard together in an attempt to force her wetness into the hard clay. Then, she took it out and placed it delicately into his mouth. Smoke poured, without much interest, from his ears. At first, that was. But slowly, as her juices ran down the stem and mixed with the tobacco in the bowl, his expression seemed to change a little. Was he hooked? She watched fascinated. Slowly, he took the pipe out of his mouth, ran his tongue up and down the stem and gave it back to her. Once again, she inserted it between her lovelips, squeezed as hard as she could and gave it back to him. This time, he sucked it long and forcefully before giving it back again. Then he repeated the whole process. After five such insertions, she noticed a change in his cock. Before, it had looked like a dead, overcooked shrimp. Now, it might just have passed for a live one. Its whole inch and a half stood erect. Once more, her teeth fastened on it and for a moment she had an inclination to bite it off, to see if it tasted of fish! But she was a good meat-eating girl. She continued to suck, while one hand played with the two little peas that lay beneath the shrimp. Would you believe it gave a little jerk and a tiny spot of come, the size of a bead of perspiration, hit her tongue? Then the shrimp faltered and died. As she got wearily to her feet, she noticed he had returned to his pipe, just as if she'd never existed.

Neither old man saw her as she dressed and then saddled her horse with its fine new toy, or saw her expression of glee as she eased her cunt over the leather ramrod. Fifteen minutes later, a fine trusty horse could be plainly seen galloping away from the saddler's workshop. The smart young girl who managed the stallion so ably had a smile like a lunatic's on her face. She'd started off from Bill and Ben's at a walk with a smile, then a trot with a grin, than a canter with a whoop of joy and when she reached the galloping stage, nothing could restrain her visage of satiated sex. Two cowboys riding by her and on into town were bemused by this eerie sight. They wondered who the hell she could be . . . It didn't enter their heads that the only thoughts she had about them was to wonder if they had big cocks!

Chapter Six

WHORE-INSPIRED

Meanwhile, Lurex Tex, quite forgetting her most recent ramble with Rose, was all of a-quiver. But for once she was not thinking of dong, dick and hairy. She was about to strike gold . . . a great big solid bulging gold vein was coming her way. She hadn't been out prospecting in the Superstition Mountains though. Her fortune wasn't coming in fat heavy nuggets, but from the come and pockets of poor sex-starved cowpokes. Lurex Tex was expanding. She had bought the dilapidated old lean-to that leant against the outer walls of her funpalace/brothel/bar. The workmen had been busy for ages. Hammering, sawing, nailing, building. But mostly screwing! She paid them in crumpet. Today would see the last nail and cock driven home. Tex walked with pride between the rough wooden benches in the auditorium of her new theatre and inhaled the sweet odours of sawdust. At this moment, it turned her on as much as the bitter-sweet smell of come. Her excitement was so great that fanny froth oozed down her thighs, all the way to her knees. She walked sedately towards the roughly-constructed stage, mounted the steps and reached out to grope the rich velvet drapes. She was very proud of these new curtains. She had imported them especially from back east. Her fingers stroked the pile and quickly ran onto her skirt. With her hand clenched in a fist, she rubbed the knuckles fiercely into her pubic bulge. The men were busy toiling with their timbers. In the gloom of the theatre, no one noticed Lurec Tex's fumblings. She was going great guns, with her head steeped in the new plush fabric. Rather sooner than later, she came. And the railroad was coming . . . Her face contorted. Staccato panting rent the air. She felt a torrent of love juice escape from her minge and roll tenderly, tearfully down her inner thigh. Moving on, she examined the backstage dressing-rooms. This was hardly a fitting description for the rabbit-hutch compartments that were built under the stage. There were four of these such holes in the wood, with no room to swing a cat in any of them. The backstage area was non-existent, for there was only about two feet between the wings and the outside wall of the theatre. An odd outdoor set had been constructed by odd outdoor workmen. A range of wobbly cardboard mountains stood but a foot from the back wall. A huge yellow orb representing the sun hung squiffy in the painted sky. To navigate from one side of the stage to the other required all the skills of a tightrope walker. Unfortunately, there were none in town. Under this primitive gangway were the steps which lead to the pokey dressing rooms. Lurex Tex was overcome once more, but this time by a great flash of pride at her fine establishment. Indeed it was quite true to say, Gold Dust, even in its boom time, had never seen the like. Tex was way ahead of her time – she was somewhat similar to a Paul Raymond of the 1800s. She had booked a touring show into her brand-spunking new theatre. She was convinced that the girls appearing on the Bill would pull in men by their pubes and wallets and make her the richest young thing in Gold Dust – which wouldn't be difficult. She hadn't seen the extravaganza she had booked herself, but its fame had spread to Gold Dust – and that fact in itself was a feat.

If Lurex Tex could have seen the miserable rabble heading away from town at that precise second, she would not have felt much elation. Arnie Fly's Wild Wild West Show was not a whore-inspiring sight, as it travelled the dusty long trail. Mr. Fly himself was bright yellow – it wasn't jaundice, he was Chinese. He had slit eyes, like sideways dollar signs. His round usually benign face was set at this time in a grim expression. He drove the first of the troupe's two waggons, hoping against hope that he had not lost his way again.

Navigation was not Arnie's forte. The waggons had once been smart and shiny as new buttons on a cavalry person's uniform. The yellow paint on the side of Arnie's mobile was now peeling and chipped. And you could only just make out its lettering – 'Arnie Fly and his Wild Wild West Show, starring Miss Wild West herself in person and live.'

On the seat next to the entrepeuneur sat one of the ladies of the show. (The term lady is used very loosely in this context.) This bleach-blonde flippitygibbet had been given the nickname of Miss Clitoris Allsorts by the other girls in the troupe. She had thick dead-straight hair (the only straight thing about her) cut in a Cleopatra fringe. She was wearing what looked like the remains of a dress after a heavy rape. But, in fact, it was one of her own designs. She sewed for herself. It was a sort of hit and miss affair in cotton. It missed a great deal more than it hit. But then Miss Allsorts was a peculiar creature. It was said by those that knew her that she had been in more beds than a packet of seeds. A mistress at the art of upstaging, she was not at all popular with the other girls, and was always trying to ingratiate herself with the yellow peril. That's why she always travelled on his seat. Miss Allsorts wanted desperately to be a star and naively thought her way to stardom was though her cunt. Her pussy had done its fair share of purring but there she was, still firmly in the chorus. She did, however, have an occasional solo guitar spot, but she continually plucked her diamente G-string, and was not a resounding success.

Sitting in the back of Arnie's waggon, her big chubby cheeks flushed by the heat, was Miss Hilda Burger. Now, she was a wow with a needle! Arnie rather grandly called her his wardrobe mistress. The fact that she was colour blind was a great hindrance. The Show's costumes were gaudy and clashed spectaculary with each other.

Lying down beside Hilda, in the most piss-elegant pose, was the star of the show – Miss Wild West, a tiny-waisted amply-busted lady. Thick dark curls sprouted in great profusion around her pale oval face. She had very slender arms and ankles. The theatrical lady used all her assets to great effect, as she sang and danced on the boards. Her eyes were big luminous pools of blue.

Wild was feeling the heat. The constraints of her corset were making breathing difficult. She fanned her fan with a small white lace hankie and prayed that, just this once, Arnie could be travelling in the right direction. She couldn't take much more of this humping and bumping. The rest of the players were crammed into the other waggon. They comprised a troupe of girls in gay mood and the master of ceremonies, Wee Winkle, a kinsperson of Arnie, and a real ham hactor (sick). Even in this heat, he sat in his Dracula-type theatre cloak and top hat. The warm winds of the prairie had affected the gum which held his huge moustache to his upper lip. It looked like some monstrous creepie-crawlie sliding down his face. The twelve wholesome girls sang to keep up their spirits. It was a little ditty they had composed over the years of travelling unecessary miles in the wrong direction with Arnie. Song:

My name is Arnie Fly
At touring I'm an ace
I know the time of get-ins
But I never know the place.

Arnie winced (as *I* used to)* as the singing floated towards him.

Hilda Burger screamed. An arrow had pierced the centre of her most outrageous bonnet.

The Indians were upon them in an instant. They swooped down from a bluff which overlooked the trail that the misguided Arnie had taken.

Whooping and screaming, their arrows soon made the waggons look like two huge pairs of airtex knickers. They circled the slowly-moving train and closed in on it, until all the terrified occupants could see was an ocean of feathers and warpaint. Hilda Burger remarked innocently 'Oh look, it's a

* See previous book 'The Story of I.'

group of the Gold Dust Amateur Theatrical Society welcoming us to the community.'

Her remark passed by without comment from the others. But Clitoris Allsorts felt in her unhinged minge, that a shag was in order. She had already spotted the brave – very brave he'd have to be – whose totem pole had taken her fancy. Hilda Burger gave forth at this moment another of her worldly comments: 'Oh look, they've got dirty feet, they must be the Blackfoot tribe.' It was when poor Hilda's ears had been pierced together by passing arrows, that the unfortunate creature realised there was nothing amateurish about this tribe. They were professional Apache and unfriendly to boot.

By now, the waggons were heading up that oft-travelled (at least in this book) trail in the dead-end direction of the mighty Superstitions. The miserable bunch were cowering in their covers, when they perceived a slight obstacle ahead. They were heading straight for a solid wall of stone with just a few prickly cacti for decoration.

A lone hang-glider passed overhead as they careered into the crevice.

It was at that moment that a bugle blared and the Fourth Cavalry came over the hill. And what a mess they made!

Chapter Seven

DICK FLASHES HIS FOOLISHNESS

Meanwhile, Dead Eye Dick wasn't very bright but he was very angry. He sat in his camp up in the hills to the east of Gold Dust and surveyed the miserable trio that was the remains of his gang.

Fatso was as his name implied; horrendously overweight. This giant mountain of blubber had a head the size of a pin. His hair grew in odd stubbly patches all over his miniscule dome. The back of his head was a thick wedge of fat which completely hid his collar. His tummy hung down like a giant beachball way over his gunbelt. He'd not seen his feet for years. And as for his privates . . . His legs were short shapeless bowed trees of excess flesh tucked into his boots. He was so slow on the draw that even he, as slow as he was, could have got to his victim before the bullet. Next to blubberpants sat Pedro. One of his eyes had ceased to function years before. Not only was he dead slow on the draw, he rarely hit anything at which he aimed. Give him a blank wall to shoot at and he'd miss it. Armless made up the threesome. So called because he was totally harmless, he was as thin as Fatso was obese. Thin sticks served as his legs. Long skinny arms hung way down below his knees. He didn't have to swing his arms down to reach his gun, but up – not an easy task for any man and Armless wasn't any sort of man at all! He didn't rate high in the shooting stakes. This bedraggled band was all that was left of Dead Eye's gang of bandits. Dick thought sadly that these dregs resembled a gaggle of ghouls far more closely than a slick troupe of outlaws. He was right.

The cause of Dick's great anguish was a sombrero, a poncho and a thin cigar. The scent of orange blossom hadn't got to him yet . . . The-Man-With-No-Voice was Dick's most hated enemy; for it was he who had captured and humiliated the ten other roughnecks who had been Dick's partners in crime. They'd gone like the pushovers they were – every one. Each time the outlaws had returned to their hideout, after some heinous escapades, one of their number would be missing presumed dead. The lost men, however, had eventually turned up, days later sometimes, like the bad pennies they were. One by one, they had been turned over to some sheriff, somewhere, always naked across their mount and delivered to the lawman's door by No-Voice. Dead Eye spat in the sand. His brain hurt. There wasn't much in his head and putting his small amount of grey cells to work caused him great pain. Why, he wondered, had he been left with these three horrors. No-Voice had had ample opportunity to knock them off – Dead Eye was always leaving them hanging around in dangerous places on the off-chance that they would be taken. But no. No-Voice only took the able and good-looking from his motley crew.

He scratched his head. How could he get back at No-Voice? No one knew his whereabouts. He was never seen, except when he was bounty collecting. He always disappeared without trace. Rumour was rife but Dead Eye thought he'd got to the bottom of the mystery. The rumours abounded and ricocheted all around the valleys of Gold Dust. It appeared that No-Voice, the big macho man, had a mini-harem of three who worked under him! Dead Eye looked at his three – God had not been kind to him. He'd swop his faded trio any time! He sighed. No-Voice had all the luck. Fortunes from bounty hunting and lovely women to amuse him in his leisure hours. What did he, Dick, the great bandito have? Nothing. Just what he deserved . . .

But Dick would never see that. He had an excessively high opinion of himself as a brave and clever man. A man whose name brought terror to the hearts of all people. It was bad luck, not bad management, that he always robbed banks, the coffers of which had just been emptied. After years of the outlaw life he had nothing to show for it but Fatso, Pedro and Armless. Hate welled up in his stocky little body. There must be some way he could strike No-Voice where it hurt. He was determined to track down the saintly hunter. He'd discover his loot, steal it – and his bevy of nubile assistants too. It was generally agreed in Gold Dust circles that No-Voice used his trio of tarts for far more than just recreational purposes. It was thought, but had never been proved, that the three bints would lure the bounty to No-Voice's lair by the very power of their sex. Outlaws then got clobbered, stripped, ravaged and despatched to the law for their trouble.

Dick was determined he would be top-dog. Although he'd heard that No-Voice would never use his weapon, Dick was still reluctant to face him in a straight gunfight. Dick was a man of many vacant thoughts and little action. He was renowned for it. He egged others into acts of violence but was Mr. Original Chicken himself. He sat and clucked in the shade of a cottonwood tree and scratched in the dust for worms of inspiration.

It was at this moment that things became a little confused. At first Dick didn't know what was going on but his band of cretins had gone ape and were pointing and gesticulating with arms and legs and anything else to hand. The swift-witted Dick gaped at these semaphoring loonies. It was then that he heard it. The rattle of the simple snake. He froze, as the asp slithered over the dry earth towards him. It stopped a foreskin's-breadth away from his person. It coiled there, eyeing him quizzically.

Far more rigid that his ramrod had ever been, he rasped: 'Do something, you bastards.'

And the bastards did. They reached for their guns as best they could – which wasn't very well at all. After the longest draws in the West, the three handguns were out. Now came the complicated part. Shooting at a small static target proved difficult for them. After a round each – and they politely took it in turns – not a bullet had nicked the wily wriggler. Dick, in a stupefied sweat, could not believe this latest incompetence. They were the pits. Ignoring the addled spermheads, he hatched a plot all of his own. He had noticed, quite by chance and out of the corner of his eye, a large sturdy stick lying on the ground only inches away from him. He stealthily edged towards the weapon and inched his hand down to pick it up. He knew he'd made a mistake as soon as his fingers wound round its rubbery thickness. His heart skipped a beat, as yet another rattler, this one not so simple, reared its ugly fangs. Throwing caution to the wind and the snake to the grass, he turned and fled, dodging the bullets that were falling like hailstones from his henchmen's irons. In mid-flight, he suddenly remembered the old wooden tin whistle that his friend Sitting Puffing Bill had given him for an occasion such as this. He whipped it out of the deep pocket in his shirt and placed the instrument to his trembling lips. He blew as though his life depended on it, which it did. The snakes recoiled in horror, danced a little jig and left asp in asp up the dusty trail. Having got rid of the leathery duo, he now had to turn his talents towards the terrible triplets. They were still convinced that danger lurked behind every boulder and were shooting indiscriminately to prove it. Dead Eye Dick lay on the ground and waved his arms and legs in rage. His hysterics soon quietened the troublesome triumverate. They stopped banging off bullets and spent the next five minutes trying to get their guns back in their holsters. Fatso let off one lonely bullet in his attempt and the other two farted in fright. As this musical symphony ceased, an idea began to form in Dick's befuddled brain.

All he had to do was to find some way to get No-Voice into trouble. That shouldn't be difficult. He'd had enough practice in getting himself into trouble. If he discredited the bounty hunter, then he'd have to do very little work. The law could take over for him. But how to do that? Suddenly it came to him. Not easily. No-Voice, reputedly, had three accomplices and so did Dick. There, all similarities in the two gangs ended. But not in the devious Dick's mind. A blinding flash of brilliance almost killed him. But at last he had it and would soon give it to his trio. There was no doubt in his mind that he could pass for the elegant easy-rider, No-Voice. But he was somewhat concerned about the other three's impersonations. It would be difficult to turn them into three luscious specimens of womanhood. But he was undeterred. He felt that with adequate make-up and a good coutourier, he could do it. After all, he was a brilliant bandit. And he would overcome these three seemingly insurmountable problems. His face cracked into a smile that was both painful and unusual, as he called his men over for a chinwag.

The moon was high in the sky as four horsemen approached Gold Dust. On the outskirts of the snoozing town, the four riders dismounted, and tied their steeds to a rail that was conveniently close by. The grotesque shadowy shapes continued their journey on foot. Their gait was ugly in the moonlight, as they crept as silently as they could from building to building. A light wind had got up, and blew the occasional small snowball of tumbleweed through town. Somewhere a door banged to and fro in the breeze. Otherwise all seemed still in hicksville.

The four mysterious men crept through the stillness. Dick and his creeps were up to no good. They were executing stage one of the Discredit-No-Voice campaign. Dick was in his disguise already. He looked perfect in his role as the bounty hunter. Except that there were two feet missing off his height! Hidden in the depths of a wooly poncho, with sombrero and cigarillo topping the deception, he prayed that the moon would go in. The furious four were on their way to Lurex Tex's parlour with intent to steal. They needed enough women's clothes to cover their ugly spreading bodies for part two of their audacity. With Dick posing as No-Voice, he would lead a raid on the town's bank, accompanied by his three trusty sidekicks dragged to the eyeballs. Then No-Voice would be on the wanted list. And Dick would reign supreme in the barren wilds of the backwater state.

Part One, unfortunately, had a major flaw, which at that moment was being ploughed by yet another potent prick.

That Tex was wide open and raring to go 24 hours a day had never occurred to witless Dick. Not for one moment did he think a lady of the night might be at her busiest in the wee small hours. Then, thinking wasn't a process that his brain cell managed desperately well. He felt sure that the damsels at LT's fun palace would be in the land of nod. The tall ramshackle wooden building was in darkness. All the downstairs windows were heavily curtained and closed tight. This was where the good time girls got their oats. Madame Tex had one of her fine apartments on the floor above and this was where the hapless quartet headed. The curtains billowed out in the night air. Yes, the window was open. The quads stood at the bottom of the building, wondering how they could attain such heights. They had nothing of use between them. But it was Armless who came to their rescue. He threw an arm up and it landed with a thud on the balcony. Very soon the rest of him followed and he was able to give the others a leg up. Fatso went first, so that Armless could pull while the others pushed. And pushed and puffed and huffed. The bulbous balloon got caught under the wooden rail. He was wedged like a stuck pig. But Dick then had his best idea of the season. They should call the sheriff to assist them. This they did and it was Rosen to the rescue for the first time in his career. Luckily, the sheriff's somnambulistic state of mind prevented him from putting two and two together to make the Dead Eye Dick four. He wasn't much use anyway in their hour of need, so they returned him to his shack where he slumbered on thinking that the whole escapade had just been part of another nightmare. Pedro suddenly developed brains where his eye should have been. He grabbed the large pin from Dick's poncho and rammed it into the monstrous full-moon of Fatso's arse. Fatso was out from under the rail like a greased hog. The foursome fell through the french window into Tex's plushest suite.

Low lights burned in ornate brass lanterns at the side of a Fatso-sized bed. Grubby fingers pawed the crisp white unsoiled linen sheets that covered the downy feather mattress. They marvelled at the wonders of the brothel. The floor-to-ceiling drapes held them spellbound as they circled the room in their awe. Furnishings like this had not been part of their underpriviledged lives. Curtains were a rarity to them, and such wall and window coverings as these fairly took their bad breath away. The finely-tooled furnishings – the washstand and the chest of drawers – amazed them too and they took their time investigating the highly-polished wooden surfaces. But the one item that held them riveted was the wardrobe. It was built like a barn out of hardwood and intricately inlaid in soft, and the bandits were shocked, when they opened the cavernous doors, at its capacity. It was full to brimming of ladies bits and pieces – just what the amateur baddies needed to execute their deviations. Flushed with a little pride and excitement, they fingered the lace frillies.

Approaching footsteps wiped the smiles from their faces and the glee from their hearts. Dick, being the leader of men that he was, dived into the woody interior of the wardrobe. Pedro and Armless followed him into the dresses. Fatso was left out in the cold. He shoved his pinhead through the doorway but his gargantuan shoulders halted his progress. He yanked his head out again and looked wildly around for another place of concealment. First, he got in the bed and lay like a beached whale beneath the counterpane. But Dead Eye, aware that his compatriot could be seen, told him to get the hell out of there. He just managed to squeeze the last few inches of his fat under the huge iron bed when, who should Tex wheel in, but Bad Jake Maddon bound and gagged on a chair with wheels. Through the cracks of the wardrobe door-jamb, Dick saw this spectacle. The others, jostling for a look at the sexual extravaganza in the room, pushed and shoved Dick and he fell with a muffled thump to the floor of the closet. He'd lost his step because of a number of strange phallic-shaped *objets d'art* underfoot. Dildo's, in the vernacular.

Tex slowly moved towards Jake, unbuttoning her skirt as

she approached. She came up to where he was roped to the unusual chair and let her skirt fall to the floor. Her half-slip must have fallen because now level with his eyes was her luscious pubic mound; just visible through the skimpy French briefs that every whore worth her onions was wearing nowadays. She grabbed him by the ears and, pulling his head towards her crotch, rubbed his nose against it. He breathed in deeply and the musky sweetness of her scent sent his cock shooting down his leg like a pogo stick.

By now, the thugs in the wardrobe were scrabbling frantically for position. None of them wanted to miss a second of this Gold Dust live show.

She tugged at his trousers and popped the bone buttons open to let his dong swing up. Her pants fell to her ankles in surprise, she stepped out of them delicately and straddled the chair which held him prisoner. Then she lowered herself until her moist round fanny touched the end of his heated pole. She reached behind her and, grasping it firmly, pushed herself down its full length. She let out her breath in a long sigh, as she felt it tunnelling into her. Jake Maddon threw himself with abandon into this, his favourite sex-game. If the sheriff could see him now! Jake had never quite worked out why he liked to be dominated in sexual situations. But like it he did. He was lord and master in every other facet of his life but there was nothing he liked more than to submit to a domineering hot-blooded woman. But he was not stuck in this physical role. He could take it the other way round too. Sexually, he was a violent man. He could be dominated or could dominate. Rough sex was his turn-on. There wasn't a tender or loving streak in his entire make-up . . . or his willy wand.

Tex's jostling globes half smothered him as she rode his totem pole like a deranged Indian. Lurex knew her business and applied herself to her studies with skill, precision and cock-loving care. A tiny frown of concentration furrowed her brow, as she breathed in and out. Her pants came in short sharp breaths, like an athlete in the latter stages of a marathon. Her breathing was nothing to the wheezing that was coming from the cupboard. Meanwhile, under the bed, Fatso couldn't understand what the bleeding hell was going on. But he thought it prudent to keep quiet, until his master signalled otherwise. The only signalling that Dead Eye Dick was doing was with his cock.

Tex, lips parted, cheeks flushed, her up-tilted eyes looking straight into those of her stupefied victim, felt him thrust up to meet her downward movements. And judging the time to be right, she arched her body forward and quickened her pace to a gallop. Indistinct sounds came from the man behind the gag. His eyes held hers with a somewhat bemused look, as she flayed and pounded her way at him. Her cunt muscles gripped tight the shaft sticking up her saddle. She stiffened, straining at his bonds. The chair rocked wildly to and fro as sperm gushed from him. Tex waited patiently above him until the earthquake subsided. Then abruptly she dismounted. She wiped the tiny beads of perspiration from her brow with the back of her hand and then, kneeling beside him, took his still-swollen member between her finger and thumb and proceeded with the next stage of the task she had set herself.

'Fuck a duck,' thought Jake. 'What's she doing now?'

The crazy broad was working on his dick again without so much as a pause to wipe herself. Jake could see a pearl of spunk on the floor. It had fallen straight out of her oyster.

'Goddam,' came Jake's mumbles through the gag. 'Gimme a break, Tex!'

His prick was still sore from the last rodeo ride and his bronco was not ready for another round. But Tex clung to her task and his knob. She frigged the skin back and forth over his glans until the rod rose once more to her attentions. Leaning over him, she took it in her mouth and flicked her tongue over the salty eye in the middle. Then, breathing noisily through her nose, she sucked and slobbered and nibbled and gnawed. His eyes were nearly bulging out of his head and his pole was nearly bulging out of his crotch. Like the big, strong stud that he was, his penis puffed up with pride. Before you could say 'Bang a bandit,' he'd shot his wad into her peachy lips. As she gagged, trying not to swallow, he fired again and it squirted out from the corners of her ruby red mouth. She pulled her head away and spat his semen on the floor.

Fatso got the drift of what was happening, as a gentle spray of come spattered over his face.

Tex wiped her hand across her mouth again and seated herself in a more comfortable position on the floor in front of Jake. She scooped his balls into one hand and, he couldn't believe it, but she began another assault on his mangled member. Squeezing and massaging it until the throbbing veins filled, Tex raised it again. She nimbly started to torture this wracked slave to do its mistress' bidding. Jake felt sure that his lust had left him but it was when Tex got off her knees and licked her way up his naked body and pushed her tongue into one ear, that Jake realised he was more of a man than even he thought possible.

Dead Eye Dick, perplexed by this obscene display of butchness, leapt from the cupboard and stood growling in front of the pair. He felt that his masculinity had a right to be heard. So he lifted up his poncho and gave Tex a flash of his foolishness. Completely taken in by Dead Eye's impersonation of the romantic No-Voice, Tex's knees turned to spermola. Protesting, but unable to act, Jake found himself flying against the chest of drawers. He remained facing the wall and struggling.

Tex was delighted at this sudden new piece of manhood to be found in the woodwork. Many's the time she had fantasised about having the mysterious Man-With-No-Voice in her bed and up her cunt. Now she had him within her grasp. She layed herself open provocatively on the bed.

'I know you can't say anything,' breathed Tex. 'But after all, words would only spoil this magic moment.'

Dick couldn't believe his luck. No woman had ever lain down and revealed her silky slot to him. What was he to do?

Was this how women behaved towards No-Voice, he thought. His hatred for the hunter rose like vomit in his throat. Dick had forgotten that the object of his hatred never, ever spoke. But luckily this whole situation had rendered our bandit speechless – which was just as well for he'd never been a wow with words!

Dead Eye staggered towards the bed, his trousers flopping around his solid ankles. His face contorted in a flush of confusion anxiety and excitement. He flipped his poncho over his shoulder, and stark, bollock naked, except for his boots with their trouser cuffs around them and his gunbelt, he crashed onto the bed with all the finesse of a derailed locomotive. Fatso, still cowering under the mattress, took the full force of the blow on his adequately padded stomach. The bandit managed to get his sharpshooter out of his holster and proceeded to wave it wildly at Tex. Poor Dick was unaware that threats were unnecessary. She was lying, ready to be taken. He raised the hem of her flimsy bodice with the end of his metal barrel. As the garment was ruffled around her neck at the time, it would have been hardly a hindrance to Dead Eye Dick's entrance. Unless he was going to poke her in the adam's apple. But Tex got the message and hastily removed her last semblance of decency. She smiled, enjoying this display of male supremecy. Dick gestured so wildly that he fell off the bed. Fatso breathed a sigh of relief. Too soon! For Dick leapt back onto the bed, like a man taking to a trampoline. He fired his gun into the ceiling bringing chunks of plaster crashing onto the bed. Tex stopped being sexy, crossed her legs and became somewhat alarmed. But the rest of the brothel inhabitants, used to such outrages, thought Tex was having a louder than usual orgasm. She'd have to handle it herself.

Her hands shot to her mouth, as she sat up to watch the lunatic bound around and around the room, trailing his trousers behind him. Dick was sure this was the way to carry on in a whore's boudoir. However, his experience was meagre, as his dabblings in eroticism hadn't been plentiful.

His mad gallop stopped as suddenly as it had begun. He advanced on Tex threateningly and made her kneel before him. With a flick of the gun in his one hand to his cock in the other, he bade her take it in her mouth. She set to with a will, as only one well-versed in the art of blow-jobs can. She sucked him, flicking her tongue across his purple-eyed monster. She let him bulge out her cheek and fill her throat with his swollen meat. But, Dead Eye Dick, getting a taste for the erotics, was not to be so easily satisfied. He pulled his pudding from her with an obscene wrenching plop and indicated that she was to stand up, then touch the floor with her hands. He pushed her legs apart. Only too happy to be splayed out in this undignified fashion, Tex watched him upside-down between her legs. Old Dead Eye advanced, organ erect, unbuckled his gunbelt and tossed it on the bed with a debonair air. And once more Fatso felt pain. Meanwhile, the inhabitants of the wardrobe had made themselves comfy. They were having a quiet, very quiet, game of poker.

'I'll raise you three pairs of knickers and one dildo,' whispered Pedro.

Dick's hand grasped Tex's hips roughly and she felt his member prodding her behind. Fearful that he might choose the smaller rosebud, she reached behind her, grasped his tool and guided it into her cunt. The mammoth machine pistoned in and out, until her knees buckled. He pulled out of her, spun her around and with both hands grabbed her by the bouncing boobs. Tex knew only ecstasy, as he drew his mouth over one, then the other, sucking hard on her nipples which jumped for joy under the assault. Jake knew only pain. Misery, as he struggled in the corner. He couldn't see a thing, but even his miserable imagination was able to conjure up something in his mind about what was going on.

Dick turned the wanton woman away from him again. He gazed at her buttocks and then pushed her forward onto the bed. He made her go on all-fours. Then he sat on the floor himself and took off his boots and trousers. Fatso got a glorious glimpse of his boss's three piece suite. He blinked and turned away – the big, bashful buffoon that he was. Dick was now in his element. After all, he knew how to ride a horse, straddling a woman couldn't be that much different! So, he got a leg over Tex's back and clamped her between his thighs. She sagged under his weight and so did Fatso. He slid off her onto his knees and pulled her by her hips until her bum was pointing up at him. Still with his sombrero firmly on his head and his poncho around his shoulder, he stood on the end of the bed, inserted himself and rammed into her steaming snatch from behind. He drove his cock deep into her and out again all in one movement; amusing himself by watching the way it tunnelled into the soft willing flesh. He withdrew it fractionally each time which made a popping sound and seemed fascinated by the juices that were dropping from her manhole and onto the sheets. Then, in search of a new diversion, he took it out completely and parted the cheeks of her arse with his broad thumbs. Aiming carefully, he drew a deep breath and prepared for the ecstasy of slipping into territory unknown.

It was then that drink got the better of it. His giant probe, poised for its illegal sly entry in Tex's back door, concertinaed like a fat pink earthworm and slid harmlessly up the crease in her buttocks. He sighed like a pricked balloon – all hot air, wind and piss. Yet another mission bit the dust.

He speedily strapped on his gunbelt, quickly rearranged his poncho and got straight back into the cupboard. After breaking up the poker school, he helped himself to armful's of ladies outdoor and indoor wear and whispering, 'Follow me,' surreptitiously to his gang, left the brothel by the back passage – a favourite haunt of his! His pitiful triangle of sidekicks were somewhat bewildered by his hasty retreat. But then got themselves together and following his example were soon heading towards their horses with their spoils. It was only when Dick's balls hit the saddle that he realised, although he'd gained a fine trousseau of women's clothes, he'd left his vitals – trousers and boots – behind him. Undeterred, he led his boys from Gold Dust and they disappeared down the trail from whence they'd came.

Back in Tex's boudoir, the lady of the night still had her bum expectantly in the air, waiting for No-Voice's prod of pleasure. She would have a long wait. The railroad was coming . . . but she wasn't – this evening anyway. Peeking through her splayed limbs, she found to her consternation that the room was empty, except for Maddon on wheels. No-Voice had left as silently as he hadn't come. Though she'd heard the rustling of what she thought was his handmaiden's skirts. It was only much later that she found out it had been her own that were being rustled. But at this moment, she was just too excited that she's had contact with the great bounty hunter No-Voice and to boot, had definite proof that he did have female accomplices.

Wobbly-legged, Tex went to the window and stepped out onto the verandah. There wasn't a sausage to be seen. She craned her neck and peered up and down the main street. No-Voice had been swallowed up by the black night. She sighed and quite forgetting her former-fuck, Jake, eased her leg over the wooden rail. Love had come to Tex's life and with it frustration. She moved her hot twat up and down, seeking comfort on the well-worn wood, while the hot desert air wafted around her naked form. Fantasising in a frenzied fashion about her departed cunter hunter, she came almost immediately. And the railroad was coming . . . Her love juices fanned out in a fine spray. Marshall Clit Westwood was bent upon her nightly beat.

'Jeez, it's raining,' she thought as droplets pitter-pattered onto the wide brim of her hat. She looked up, straight into Tex's open rare orchid.

'Hi, marshall, have I got some news for you,' shouted Tex cheerfully, completely ignoring the fact that her present position may have looked a little strange to the law person.

'If Tex has had to resort to this masturbatory prank, there certainly must be something afoot,' thought Clit. She sprinted into the whorehouse, sending her chaps flying.

Taking the stairs three at a time, and not letting the muffled cries of orgasmic pleasure she passed en route deter her, she slammed open the door of Tex's shagroom and stood hands on her hips ready for anything that the madame might give her . . . in the way of information. She was about to stride across to the open window, when she caught sight of a huddled figure in a chair by the wall. The most unearthly groaning and grunting was escaping from this creature. Clit tiptoed up behind the spectre and with a flick of her wrist, spun the chair around to face her. Maddon sat there exposed. Her eyes flicked imperiously over the wretch's body and she began to giggle. She stared in disbelief that such a big man as Maddon should have such a tiny willy. But then, she didn't know what the poor little dick had been through. There was hardly an ounce of blood left in its shrunken shell. Bored with this, she turned the pathetic outlaw back to face the wall. He didn't approve of this action – she could tell. He cursed through his gag but Clit wasn't interested in gaining this bastard's approval. She left him farting and frigging about and glided with a certain air of butchness to where Tex was still impaled upon her wooden pole.

'Now what's all this ducks?' asked Clit as she removed the odd splinter from Tex's bum.

Marshall Westwood coaxed the luscious young head-whore back into the warm boudoir.

'Tell me,' implored the curious Clit, her minge a-twitter with excitement, 'what's been happening?'

'I've had a visitation from the great bounty hunter,' exclaimed Tex with surprising eloquence.

'You don't mean, surely not . . .'

'Yes, yes,' squealed Tex. 'He's been here . . . the big man . . . with no voice.'

There separate roles of marshall and whore forgotten, they became girls gossiping together. Clit pressed Tex for a detailed blow-by-blow description of her encounter. And Tex didn't need much ironing!

'He was as horny as hell,' she lied slightly. 'It was the best orgasm I've ever had,' she lied even more. 'His cock,' she enthused, now with little truth, 'was at least fourteen inches long and as wide as the Grand Canyon.'

'Hmm,' thought Clit bitchily, 'sounds like a helluva lot more fun than a poke in the eye with a stick.'

'He was circumcised,' Tex informed.

'And they threw the wrong bit away I bet,' Clit spat under her breath.

The latter could hardly conceal her raging jealousy at No-Voice picking a scrubber for his first public coming, when there were such delights as herself abroad.

Unabashed, Tex hallucinated on. 'His skin was hot and smooth as the desert wind. His husky aroma enthralled me. Under the shade of his old sombrero, his eyes were brimming with lust for me. He kissed me, yes, and my lips were consumed by fire.'

'I expect he forgot to take his cigar out,' returned Clit unecessarily.

Catching wind of Clit's fearful envy, Tex trowelled on: 'He came four times and each one was an experience more moving and earth-shattering than the one before. He was such a good lover. He filled every orifice. Before this night, I was only interested in cocks – all the inches of passion-stick I could lay my hands and cunt on. But all that is in the past. Although I'm prepared to carry on earning a crust, I will never enjoy penetration as I did in the past . . . unless it's from him.'

Clit marvelled at this mush, coming from so wanton a hole. She'd been pricked into love by the mystery of the unlawful poncho. Thoroughly sickened by the hearts and flowers spewing over the floor, Clit took her leave. She only paused in her exit to administer a playful poke to Madden's privates. His shriek of muffles pain rang out, breaking the monotony of the balmy air.

Chapter Eight

ROSE'S GYNAECOLOGY NIBBLES HER KNICKERS

Meanwhile, over at the Carsons', an argument was in full spate. Chuck had finally lured Rose back to home-sweet-home but Rose still wasn't having any. She still hated the idea that he had succumbed to rape.

'You must have egged that woman on,' wailed Rose. 'After all, how could a woman, however strong, get her leg over a great butch thing like you.'

'It wasn't like that Rose,' whined the flummoxed Chuck, 'when you're staring down the barrel of a gun, what choice do you have but to get your cock out as commanded?'

'But how,' queried Rose, 'could you get a hard-on in such unnatural circumstances?'

'But she had her hand in my knickers,' came the shocking reply. 'Her hot little paw just pulled away at my ding-a-ling. How could I stop it getting swollen headed? You know how virile I am. It just grew and grew out of all proportion, as it always does. And you know how you like it.'

He added this final remark seductively, as he backed her onto the kitchen table. But Rose still wasn't having any. So Chuck continued his heavy little number, relating everything that had gone on and hoping that the intimate details of his seduction and consequent downfall would rouse the rambling Rose to get her thorns prickly and all that . . .

'Do you know what she did then?' cried Chuck continuing, 'she ran the cold steel of her bare gun up and down my wand. It jerked under this ice-cold caress. She flicked it roughly back and forth, whilst commanding me to stay perfectly still. She hitched her skirt way up in her belt and allowed me full view of the lubricating swollen lips. Then, with her gun still levelled at my goolies, she whipped out from behind her, a three-legged wooden stool and placed it upside down on the ground almost directly under my flagpole. It was then that I noticed that the legs were bent and peculiar. Each was a perfectly-turned model of a cock, complete with large drooping balls beneath. They were of different widths and she started with the thinnest. She just sat straight on it – it fair made my eyes water. Just like a child sliding down a bannister. She spun once and before I knew what had happened, the gun was back on my bollocks. My pubic hairs stood on end. Then, she started bouncing up and down on the first stool leg, giving little yells and whoops like a jazz musician. Moisture streamed in a waterfall down the last couple of inches of the wood. Her little shouts were soon drowned out by the gushing tide. The moon beamed benignly down on us. It smiled on her endeavours and my cock. Without warning, she was upon the second sturdy piece of wood. I held my breath but the bolt shot home. Up and down she rocked, her hand still holding her piece pointed at the region of my privates. When she skewered herself on the third and fattest leg, I thought *my* third leg would burst. I had a suspicion though that I might get shot if I came and wasted my come on the barren earth. Just then a cloud obscured the moon. All went black and hairy and I bit the dust. I looked up and as the cloud passed, I saw the moon framed between her legs. It looked so pretty with its pubic fringe – a gently curling eyelash of some exotic creature. Then the lights went out again, as she lowered her furry man-eating animal onto my face. Two wet lips brushed down the bridge of my nose, over my chin and pushed their way down my chest. She plopped herself on my old man, like a district nurse getting on her bicycle. She pedalled off in all directions. I came when she got to the top of the first hill.'

Rose turned to and turned on Chuck. Far from distressing her, his confessions had got her gynaecology nibbling at her knickers. She looked at Chuck longingly for the first time in weeks. She decided not to ruin the moment by burdening him with her lesbian tendencies. There were times in a sexual relationship when a little white lie is preferable to the ugly truth. Chuck in a temper was not a thing she'd wish upon her worst enemy. She didn't want to get killed – she wanted to get fucked. In her lust, she forgave everything.

Her lips and tongue pressed wetly against his mouth. She ran her fingers up to the nape of his neck, and curled them into his hair. After a long and passionate kiss, Rose stood up, gazing steadily at him. Slowly, she unbuttoned and discarded her blouse to reveal the lush white breasts beneath. Then unhooking the clasp at her waist, she allowed the riding skirt to drop to the floor. She was naked. Chuck was pleasantly surprised, as she cheekily pointed her pubes at him. The fleecy golden mound scarcely concealed the bulging pussy beneath, and her glistening clit peeked out at him provocatively. After a brief hesitation, she knelt down beside him and fingered his fly. She undid his belt, the hook and the top buttons and, with adept fingers, she extricated his hardening knob from his pantaloons. Beneath her passionate gaze, it straightened and stood upright to her attentions. A miniscule droplet gathering in anticipation at its tip. She took it into her mouth; drawing it deep into her throat. She choked and then drew it in, sucking all the while. Chuck stood before her breathing deeply. Holding her face between his hands, he caressed the downy curve of her cheek. Abruptly, he pulled his sex plug from her mouth and, raising his wife to her feet, led her to the bedroom. They lived in a bungalow.

Rose lay down on her stomach with her face to the wall. He tentatively touched the tiny rosebud of her vulva. His thumbs slid down and into her sopping slot. He opened her wide and stared into the mystery of her sex. She oozed her delight and he buried his mouth in its full-lipped folds, making her cry out as his tongue touched the tip of her clitoral hillocks. She began to moan and thrust her buttocks upwards at his face. Naughtily, it reminded him just for a second of the full moon of his rape. His tongue drove deeper, lapping at the moist walls of her cunt. And then again he pulled away, causing her to turn over on the bed, lowering her backside as she went. She looked up at him questioningly. He placed a hand under her chin and kissed her gently. As they fused, their tongues clashed madly and her hands reached between their bodies for his cock. Hungrily, she fed it to her waiting lower orifice, and thrust herself up at him as he began to move upon her. Crushing her breasts with his weight, he quickened his pace. She wailed and trembled as he felt his own climax approaching. He lowered his head and took first one hard nipple, then the other, in his mouth. Forgetting himself, he bit her. When she cried out, he apologised and stroked it with his hand until it rose up again. His hardness speared her now with brutal jabbing thrusts and she opened herself wide to his pounding need. Their loins meshed in painful frenzy as they came together in a powerful orgasm that left him spent and drained; and gave her, wave upon wave in wonderment – cunt contracting, hips undulating, pussy pulsing, gently, long into the never-ending night.

Chapter Nine

GOOD VERSUS BETTER

Meanwhile, the Wild Wild West Show was settling into a long run at Tex's new theatre. Another opening of another show! Arnie Fly, on his arrival, had been somewhat distressed first by his recent narrow escape from death by Indians, and secondly by the knowledge that he'd made another monumental cock-up. He'd thought that it'd been the big Gold Dust – the city on the Pacific coast – not this hick hole in the desert. When his troupe had tumbled out of their much abused waggons, the thespians had appeared a little distraught, finding themselves in such a naff gaff. Ms Wild swanned in and demanded to see the number one dressing room. Tex proudly guided her to the bowels of the theatre and pointed at a long dark hole under the stage. It had a sheriff's star pinned onto the door and was merely longer and darker than any of the others. She went into a spout of the dramatics, while poor Arnie did his best to pour oil on the troubled theatrical waters. He promised, lying though his teeth, to rectify the situation as soon as he possibly could. He implored her as a true pro to put up with it for the moment, because the show had to go on that night. The troupe of twelve, Miss Allsorts and the master of ceremonies, Wee Winkle, were all shown by Tex into the middle-sized hole that served as their dressing room. They stood shoulder to shoulder and raised their eyes in the air. They were used to Arnie's blunders but even they had to admit he'd excelled himself this time! There was hardly room to swivel a cat, let alone a tit, and they had twenty-six of those. And poor Wee Winkle couldn't even flick his cape, as was his usual theatrical bent.

Hilda Burger, proud of her newly-pierced ears (!), folded her flesh and silently crept into *her* hole. She was sharing it with Arnie. She managed to get her skips in but it was a hell of an effort to raise the creaky wicker lids. But with the help of Arnie, who somehow had squeezed in there, too, she did it. There was no clothes rail however, and for seconds she was at a loss. Then she thought of Clitoris Allsorts. If anyone could get anything done, it was she. She screamed down the corridor, 'Allsorts.' and the slippery Clit snaked her way through the others in the chorus, trod on Wee Winkle and presented herself to Hilda. As usual, she was wearing nothing but her shoes. She never took her shoes off – she just didn't feel dressed without them!

'Go,' said Hilda Burger, 'whither they bang!'

The stupid girl's face lit up as she thought of another sort of banging. Hilda had in fact meant for the girl to go and get a builder to do something about the lack of rails. But Allsorts, bum quivering with excitement, had already gone. Up the steep steps she went, along the wobby platform and onto the backstage area – all one foot of it. It was here that she encountered her first workman; with his tools all over the place. Matthew Webster was hard at it. He was hammering the last few nails into the cardboard range of mountains. He looked up and wiped his brow and found he was staring at a huge furry animal on legs. It didn't take him long to recognise that this was a naked woman. He'd come a long way since his barn initiation into the ways of law and order, Clit-wise.

'Can you come?' remarked Allsorts casually.

Matthew, somewhat shocked by this unladylike interrogation, blushed. He knew perfectly well he could and by the feeling he was experiencing in his rough buckskin trousers, he would do so at any moment. Undeterred by his show of uncommunicative modesty, Allsorts thrust her stubbly pubes within an inch of Matthew's scarlet face.

'Can you come and fix a rail?'

Matthew rose to the occasion and got off his knees. He

stood facing Allsorts. She pressed her hot little body against him. Matthew felt her bright pointed nipples perforating his woolly check shirt.

'What do you mean!' he asked unnecessarily.

Taking a deep breath and twitching all over, she rubbed her nakedness into him. Her cherry red lips puckered in a dramatic pout. The heavy lids of her eyes flickered.

'I'm going to have you by the end of the week,' she hissed. 'Follow me.'

She turned on her high heels and the mesmerised Matthew followed on after the white moon of her bare arse. Allsorts led him to her dressing room and, just as he thought his luck was in, disappeared into the dark hole. She just had time to point to Hilda's hideaway. Matthew stumbled towards it to be greeted by the wardrobe mistress – plump, smiling and filling the doorway.

'Have you come to fix my rail? There's a good boy,' said Hilda, patting him on the cock in a maternal fashion.

Matthew quickly learnt that Hilda could not make decisions. No sooner had she decided to put her rail in one spot and Matthew had started hammering than she said,

'Oooh, I think it would more aesthetically pleasing over there.'

Matthew kept his cool and eventually it was put in the very first place he had had it. Hilda thanked the boy.

'For that,' she said, 'I'll give you a ticket for the front row at the opening tonight.'

Matthew who'd only been to one opening – and that was not a theatre's – was thrilled to the root of his rod and came again in his trousers.

He went back to his job, finished it in double quick time and took his seat in the front row. It was only three o'clock in the afternoon and the show wasn't due to start until ten that evening . . . Tex, in an effort to drum up custom, had taken to the streets – or rather the girls had, under her instruction. They'd donned sandwich boards and very little else and were at that moment stalking the streets of Gold

Dust. Shouting 'Roll-up, roll-up,' the floosies were having a whale of a time. The male inhabitants of Gold Dust looked quite excited when they managed to read what was on the boards. This took quite some time for them, because they seemed to be far more interested in the near-to-naked creatures underneath. The boards screamed at the people:

'Best show in town.'
'Naughty but nice.'
'Come and come at the new theatre.'
'Get your rocks off down at Tex's glitter palace.'
'Nude women, a funny man and lots, lots more.'
'No hold barred – you'll never believe your eyes.'
'The show they said could never open.'

The townswomen, led by dear sweet Rose, were quite affronted by this audacious idea of Tex's. They quickly formed an action committee and ran up a few banners of their own. These read not half as attractively:

'Down with Tex.'
'No to nudes.'
'Down with porn.'
'Goodbye sex.'

Round and round the righteous band went and finally came to rest on the steps of the newly-built theatre. It was here, and some might say it was a seemingly inappropriate place, that they decided to hold their first prayer meeting. The women were a sorry bunch, not an appetising lot – all except sweet Rose that was. They looked like they had stepped out of a Giles cartoon. They'd all gone to seed, never looked after themselves and the seasons and elements had ravaged their features. Their little get-together consisted of hours and hours of prayer, in which the prosaic ladies asked their God for a sign. Lo and behold the heavens opened and the drought in Gold Dust was over! It peed down. Torrents of cats and dogs. And the water washed the ladies from the steps and they sailed like a flotilla of large battleships down the street. Mrs. Carson rose up from the quagmire, which by now came up to her knees, and she started to shout her protests at Lurex Tex. The latter had come out onto the verandah of her bawdy house to see what all the fuss was about. She opened her mouth to phrase a question of the Christian band, when a large ball of mud hit her *splat* in the middle of her face. The mud-caked Tex could not believe what had come to pass. The other righteous ladies, following Rose's muddy example were rolling balls in their hands preparing to bombard the unfortunate whore. Not only was it now raining sheets of water, but the air was thick with mucky missiles of wet earth. Tex began to seethe. She flung a leg over the rail and slid down one of the supporting posts, having a quick orgasm en route to the ground. She landed with all the aplomb of a piece of Skylab. Before the lurid Tex could rise to her ankles, a mud-streaked bat was upon her.

'Oooh, vampires,' she thought, offering her neck with a shiver of delight.

But this was no vampire, this was Rose. Like a crazed animal, she drove her claws into Tex's curious coil. The hair fell out of the loop and over her face. She retaliated by ripping the front of Rose's blouse, until it hung in tatters on the young girl's frame. Rose got her own back by getting her slim fingers in the waistband of Tex's skirt. She gave an almighty heave and, with a dreadful ripping noise, the piece of clothing parted company from its owner. Rose stamped on it in the mud, adding insult to injury. It was ironic that the two girls should now be brawling in the streets, when their last encounter had been so tender and loving. The two grappled violently with each other and fell in the morass. Rose got her hands inside the delicate material of Tex's knickers. She merely pulled outwards, the elastic creaked and groaned and it finally gave way. The knickers shot to the ground, like a rocket from a launching pad. Next off came the blouse. Before Tex could get her own back, Rose had her blouse in shreds. Tex stood there, breasts heaving and covered with ugly streaks of dirt. The pair were by now encircled by a very large group of engrossed Gold Dusters. Rose kicked her assailant below the belt and she fell to the ground. Cheers went up as Tex, oozing filth, rose like the monster from the blue lagoon and flung herself at the deputy sheriff's wife. Tex lunged forward and pinned Rose to the dirt. She sank almost without a trace. But Tex wasn't having Rose drowning on the job. She caught hold of her flaying arms and yanked her back to the surface. Rose's pretty features were obscured by a mudpack – long before they were invented! Tex, by now, resembled a chocolate-covered jelly baby. She was covered from head to foot in a thick layer of slime. And she was very angry. Tex felt that Rose was getting the better of her in this murky fracas. She moved towards the younger woman, looking for all the world like the Incredible Hulk. Her arms went around Rose's slight supple form and she gave the girl a bare hug.

'Take me I'm yours,' she whispered in a coarse voice.

Rose was enraged by this affront. Tex was trying to give her a leg-over in the mud . . .

'Sod off, you lesbian cow,' hissed Rose, jabbing her sharp elbow into the soft easy flesh of Tex's tummy.

At this, Tex was spurred to greater heights of viciousness. She reached out a hand and caught Rose's left boob in her palm. Her fingers twisted the nipple around, as though she was trying to unscrew it. Rose shrieked in agony, terrified she's be nippless for the rest of her life. And Chuck did so like her little breast buds. She fought back by getting a handful of Tex's thick curly pubes. She almost pulled the skin from her mound, which raised in gooseflesh at the inhuman treatment. Tex wailed as her pubes received this punishment. Still with her hand menacingly on the young girl's tit, Tex dropped her other hand and clasped the hem of Rose's once-white organza skirt. Abruptly pulling away from Rose's mammaries, she caught the material of the skirt between both hands. She gave a tremendous tug and the fabric rent in two, exposing the fact that Mrs. Goody-Goody had been knickerless in the streets of Gold Dust.

Screaming 'You whore,' in surprise, Tex lost her footing in the bog. She fell over backwards and the next thing she was conscious of was Rose's soft form pressing into her own. But this was no love tussle – the young girl was still fighting like a tigress. Clit Westwood, spurs-a-jangling came squelching through the mud.

'This is no way for women to behave,' said the fierce and awesome marshall.

With that, she pulled the tiny rosebud from the big brown Tex. She got them both to their feet and was preparing to give them a dressing down and a dressing up, when she suddenly saw the funny side of the situation. She smiled at the two newly-tinted persons and said: 'Hullo dere, I's your nu marshall!'

Tex and Rose thought that this remark was about as funny as diptheria. Looking at each other, they suddenly found between them a new sisterhood and threw old bossyboots into the quagmire. Another cheer went up from the amazed spectators. Spurred on by this encouragement, the two fell upon a Clit. Six legs thrashed from beneath the waves, like a giant octupus in the throes of copulation. The girls were having a wow of a time. Fingers found all sorts of holes. As quickly as it had begun, the rain ceased. In no time at all, the hot sun dried up the moisture in the ground and turned the mud into cakes of clay.

The three women set hard. As they rose, the mud stiffened in the sun. They were stuck in these moulds of dry earth. They couldn't move. They stood against the skyline like three erotic primitive African carvings.

The townspeople wandered off satisfied with the show and leaving the performers to their just desserts. The trio of mudcases were not at all amused. In fact they were desperate. So caked were they, that they couldn't even open their mouths to beg for help. Jake Maddon had been watching the bizarre spectacle with great interest. He was particularly interested in one of the three.

'And now I've got her,' he thought wickedly.

Acting immediately, he sent Sheriff Rosen to scoop up Clit from her sun-baked pedestal. The other two grizzly shapes made distraught noises, as Rosen made off with Maddon's pat-a-cake. Following his master's instructions, he hosed her down in the back yard of the jail, threw her some of her own clothes, which he'd stolen from her bag and trussed her up like the plump tasty chicken that she was. Omitting the stuffing – he wasn't very deft with sage and onion – he delivered her to Maddon's ranch. Once there, the baddie took control of her. Rosen was despatched back to town and the outlaw took time to savour his succulent prize. He had prepared his little game well and very quickly. They were alone, now, a few miles from Gold Dust and no one would disturb them. He surveyed his prisoner. Marshall Clit Westwood was clear-complexioned, high breasted and full lipped. She had all the attributes that go to make a desirable woman. But try as he might, Jake Maddon found himself unable to respond to her. He was amazed that not an inch of his cock had risen to a millimetre of her minge. Her unflinching gaze, the contempt in the curl of her luscious mouth, froze his sexual prowess as effectively as if he was lying at the bottom of an iced-up mountain stream, with two tons of rock tied to his balls. He was very angry. Clit smiled – a thin, deadly smile. Hog-tied as she was, she still managed to arch her back and project her tits at him like proud six-shooters. He felt his scrotum shrivel. Damn the woman! And he stomped off to where their horses were tethered together to fiddle with his harness while he tried to collect his wits. Not an easy thing for Jake Maddon to do at this point in time. He was so used to being in command, except when tied up by Tex. But now he was top dog and somehow Clit, even bound like this, made him feel that she was the mistress and he the slave. Goddam, she was a puzzle. Thinking about her now, without those eyes on him, he felt the lust flow back into his loins. He stiffened like a Winchester barrel, at the prospect of tearing off her riding breeches and ramming her sassy snatch. His cock, rigid and ravenous, pushed its way up under his gunbelt at the thought of what he could do to her. They were still alone and miles from civilisation, with nothing but mountains and desert around them and nobody and nothing to stop him splitting this tasty chicken down the middle with his barbecue stick. Almost shooting his bolt with lust, he turned towards the marshall. He tore open the crotch of his trousers and followed his bobbling tool to where she lay, tied and helpless. Not daring to look at her face, he scrambled up to her on all fours, his gunbelt trailing in the dirt. Her ankles and wrists were bound together and he was going to have to figure a way of getting her pants down. This posed quite a problem for cretinous Jake. He didn't dare untie her or admit he was frightened of her. Still his cock was firm with resolve and the spunk boiled in his boilers. This time he would have her. Otherwise his name wasn't Jake Maddon. Neither it was. He'd been christened Cecil Droopers. Grabbing her by the ankles, he flipped her over with a powerful twist, that left her panting face down in the dirt. Her rounded rump filled her breeches tight to bursting. He tugged with trembling hands at the buckle around her slim waist. The belt undone, he pulled at the trousers and tried to ease them down over her hips. But tied up as she was, there was no way the waistband would come down past her knees. Groaning with frustration, his great purple knob getting in the way, he heaved and pulled and jerked at her garments, in a desperate bid to poke the prettiest piece of ass he'd ever seen. Clit lay coiled and still as a cobra, waiting for the badman's first false move. As his paws began fumbling again with her clothes, she felt his heated shaft bouncing against her midriff. Her eyes were two slits filled with hate. She tensed her whole body, clenching her fists to make his path as darn near impossible as dammit. Jake the Rake was beside himself with what to do. Her bare arse, peeping above her pants was driving him mad with desire. He had the hots for this woman. His joint was burning like a branding iron. And his sex-crazed brain could see that his only hope was to cool it in the liquid insides of his victim. Her mouth! That was it. He'd plant it in her mouth. And that's what did it. The thought of it took him over the edge. With the safety catch off, his prick and balls became a pump-action carbine, banging off on their own, jerking his buttocks in the air in a series of mule kicks. His seed sprayed out in sizzling spurts onto the sand. Jeez. He caught Clit's imperious look and choked with rage, as she licked her lips and smiled knowingly. His coming was his undoing and hers. Matthew had vacated his front row seat, knowing that his first love as in danger. He had followed hot on Clit's clit. He'd sniffed her steamy scent and tracked her to this hell-hole. He'd witnessed Jake's shame and prem ejac from behind a boulder. Jake's eyes were too glazed to see the lad's stealthy approach, his senses still reeling from his recent come. He hardly felt the blow that fell upon his already-thumping head. Matthew, as sure and quick footed as a young deer, sprang to Clit's aid. He gently pulled off her trousers and undid the cutting bonds. She rubbed her hands and his cock gratefully. 'Aaah,' she sighed. She had no time for pleasure pricks now.

Jake needed seeing to. He awoke tied to a mule and charging towards Gold Dust. One more baddie had been captured by pussy galore. For Marshall Clit, sex was the soft solution of keeping law and order. There was nothing like it for subduing a man. And she had to admit from time to time, it gave a measure of enjoyment to her work. Now she had captured another quarry, she felt the familiar tingle start up at the junction of her thighs. Encased in the official leather of her profession, the cheeks of her arse slapped rhythmically against the hard smooth saddle. She leaned forward at a gallop and brought her clit against the pommel: Up, down, up down. The tingling became a burning and the embers flickered into a flame, as she lashed the beast beneath her and lead Jake Maddon, the no-good, mother-fucking son of a bitch into town. Matthew, as usual, had had a hard job keeping up with the Marshall's racey pace. He rounded a bend to find her sitting in a heap in the dust. There was no trace of Maddon . . .

Chapter Ten

LIQUORICE ALLSORTS

Meanwhile, all was not well upon the boards at Tex's opening night. The hall was packed, no doubt because of the mud-wrestling publicity, with liquor-crazed cowpokes. If a cow had been passing, anyway, they probably would have poked it! Backstage, all was not right either. In fact, it was a helluva mess in the one foot of stage that the player's had to use to prepare themselves for the show. The orchestra struck up, or rather the man on the piano did. He was playing the most peculiar band parts. He had nobody's key in mind in his tuneless ramblings and Tex got hot under the collar at the thought that she may have made a big mistake at his audition. He smiled a lot and flicked his hair. Tex sweated. He launched into the show's overture but his masterpiece was cut in mid-crochet by the appearance of R. Sole or, as he was known in the trade, Wee Winkle, struggling to get out through the curtains. The poor man was not adept at finding holes and the curtains bulged and billowed as he grappled with their live folds. But finally he was out, and you could tell by the reaction of the audience that most of them wished he hadn't bothered. This wasn't what they'd come for. He started on his lonely soliloquy to cries of 'Get them off,' and 'Show us your tits.' Wee, in this desperate moment, used his one and only ad-lib.

'I've looked up the definition of heckler in my trusty dictionary,' he opened bravely. 'And, surprise, surprise, the definition is baiter.'

Selecting Matthew at random from the front row (he'd rushed back for curtain-up), Wee launched into the punch line:

'And you sir, are a Master Baiter.'

Matthew, who'd jerked off on the way into town with Clit, was still not used to this sort of sexual badinage. He tried to bury himself under his hard wooden bench. He blushed, while the audience pointed and laughed at him. During this ribaldry, Winkle had vanished and, with a great effort, the curtains had parted to reveal an empty stage. From the wings cries of 'Get on,' could plainly be heard. Hilda Burger backed on, fully clothed, and was barracked with bullets. She backed off again immediately. The pianist, sensing something was amiss, launched into a very ambitious (for him) piano concerto. This little piece was played entirely on the white keys and did not benefit from that fact at all . . . The first turn out was Allsorts, who seemed to have her knees tied to her ears with elastic. Flushed with pride that she suddenly had a solo spot opening the show, the poor girl could do nothing but what she was famous for. She crouched there, plucking her g-string on the guitar with not a care in the world.

Behind the scenes, havoc reigned, with Hilda Burger in control! Miss Wild, sequins and feathers all of a-flutter, was preparing to launch herself from the wings. She was determined to bring Allsorts' number to a close. She swept on with a faintly regal air, dragging Miss Hilda Burger who was sewing a piece of boa onto her clothes at the time. A yellow arm shot out and grasped Hilda by the neck. And she was off.

Miss Wild looked like an erotic chicken – brilliant orange feathers had been woven into her tresses. She minced imperiously up and down in front of Miss Allsorts, swirling her large black boa-trimmed cloak in her face. Allsorts was not put off. She peered around the corners of the cloud of fluff and smiled at the audience with her lower pink lips. This was a well-worn up-staging trick she'd used again and again. So, while Wild was battling to gain the attention of the audience with her sultry singing, Allsorts was flashing her wherewithal behind the songstress. At one point, she even managed to walk across the stage on her vaginal legs. Wild was a great star and fine performer. She kept working her cloak and obliterating the miserable minge behind her. A long walking stick with a long handle snaked onto the stage from the wings, caught Allsorts around the neck and snaked off again with her in its grip. She howled as she went. Now Wild had the stage to herself, she certainly lived up to her name. She went wild, to the watusi music coming from the piano. Gyrating and throwing her head back and forth, she tried to grip the audience with her sexual vibrations. She ran her fingers up the inside of her stockinged legs and toyed with the decorative black lace of her suspender. The cowboys joined in the chorus, although there wasn't one.

'Get em off,' one of them yelled originally.

Wild replied: 'I don't think they'd fit you, cowboy.'

One heavily-pissed hoodlum kept up a constant stream of wisecracks. It seemed to amuse him no end. Wild floored him with a few fast strokes of her tongue.

'Why don't you sit against the wall – that's plastered too,' she barked.

The pisspot muttered again.

'You and I,' retorted Wild, 'should do a double act.'

A look of delight spread across the idiot's face.

'Yes,' she continued, 'I'll sing Swanee River, and you, you pillock, can jump in it.'

The others in the audience roared their approval, raining bullets over their heads and into the ceiling. The nuisance kept at it.

'You're such a smart-arse,' said Wild, 'I suppose you could sit on an ice cream and tell me what flavour it is.'

Not at all deflated, the joker oozed words of derision.

'OK, OK, stand up you dude,' Wild spat. 'And let's see if the rest of you is as big as your mouth.'

The offender lurched drunkenly to his feet and tried vainly to unleash his pink prawn. The effort appeared to be too much for this strapping big man. He sank slowly to his arse and slid with a sad little burble under the bench and onto the floor. Wild went on with her routine without any more backchat or interference from the cowhands in the auditorium. One lout, however, rested his huge dirty boots on the edge of the stage. Miss Wild sidled up to him in her most seductive manner. Hand on the hip, she pouted at him prettily. He, thinking his luck was in, winked at her. She knelt down on the edge of the stage and caressed his boots lovingly. In a low sexy voice, she asked him 'Are you in show business, mister?'

'Why, no,' replied the big hulk.

'Then, get your friggin' feet off the fuckin' stage.'

Her sensitive feminine teasing brought the house down. Tex was very worried in case the insurance premiums hadn't been paid.

Allsorts and the girls came on high-kicking in a line, behind Wild. As usual, Allsorts had left off her drawers. And it was step, tap, ball-change, kick, minge-a-gogo. The rest of the girls, infuriated by her flashing, moved surreptitiously around her, until she was smiling and bopping at the end of the line. Then they all stepped very firmly towards her. Allsorts found her self going tit-over-heels down the stairs. She landed with her head in a half-empty skip. Hilda Burger, who was feeling particularly vicious at that moment, slammed the lid down on the girl's head. When Allsorts surfaced from the musty interior of the wicker chest, she'd stopped flashing and smiling.

'Hmm,' said Hilda, staring at the girl's ravaged countenance, 'your face has had more lifts than a lavatory seat.'

She chuckled madly to herself and continued knitting a winkle warmer for the winter. Hilda had hundreds of them, all sizes, shapes and colours. She liked to have a second string to her bow and, if her theatrical career came a cropper, she would be ready to open a kinky clothes shop anywhere. Allsorts, quite out of sorts, crawled back into the hole she'd come out of, nursing a fearful headache. On the boards above, Wild and the girls were taking their fifteenth curtain call. Tex, still with bits of mud about her person, was counting the evening's take. If she got this sort of crowd every night, she would be able to retire in a fortnight and settle down in marital bliss with No-Voice!

Chapter Eleven

AN INDIAN . . . SUMMER . . . TALE

Meanwhile, Dead Eye Dick's whole body was rigid with excitement. His band of banditos looked at him with new eyes. They hadn't realised the extent of Dick's sexual prick-prowess, until they'd seen him *sur le travail* with Tex. Every day, since his beautiful bunk-up, he'd ordered his gaggle to stay at camp and guard their paltry belongings. He'd religiously ridden into Gold Dust every 24 hours, in yet another of his spell-binding disguises. He'd watched the comings and goings at the bank all this time. And every evening, he'd watched the staff leave and the manager lock up. He'd been at it a fortnight, when one Friday towards sunset, a buggy arrived in front of the bank. Two huge cowpokes bristling with hardware guarded the door, while several sweating bank employees carried a large metal box out of the building and placed it in the back of the horse-vehicle. The musclemen got in with the goodies and sat their bums heavily upon the safe. Dick's heart pounded and his palms itched furiously, as he thought of the money that would soon be his.

His head hurt these days, as he worked feverishly on his plot to get rich and discredit No-Voice all in one thrust. Then, he could reveal his true identity to Lurex Tex and become King of her little castle. What he didn't know, however, was that at the precise moment he was watching the safe loaded into the cart with the two henchmen, the real money was going out of the bank by the back door in saddlebags with an express rider.

During this time, Dick had laid his plans carefully and had taken his dumb trio through their paces again and again.

Fatso had fallen away in lumps, or rather, had slimmed down to an acceptable weight. He'd been on a diet of three beans a day and was looking almost svelte – though he'd never be pretty. Pedro, Fatso and Armless had been plodding around their backyard for weeks now in their women's weeds. Dick was nothing if not thorough and had insisted that his boys get used to their new clothing. They were a truly amazing spectacle. Armless was in a skin-tight bodice, with the hairs of his chest sprouting wildly over the top. His shapeless bottom-half was encased in a divided riding skirt. Legs like two upturned milk bottles stuck out from beneath the hem. Fatso resembled a deflated beach ball in his striped number. He bagged and sagged as he waggled and walked. Clever Pedro had found a diamente g-string in the bag of goodies. He thought it was an eyepatch and sported it nattily over his long-gone optic. He couldn't work out why it had such a strange perfume! It was Tex's best. The rest of him was tucked into an affair of white linen. He looked super and Dick almost fancied him in this rig-out.

The day came for Dead Eye's plan to grind into action. Far from being concerned that the three others wouldn't be able to pull off their female roles in this raid, he was now perturbed that they would lose what little machismo they had ever had and continue their life of transvestitism. But he wasn't really going to worry about their cross-dressing welfare, once he had his hands on the loot.

So, the hideous quartet grouped themselves thus, before setting off near sundown one Friday for the fray. They mounted, three sidesaddle and one astride, and set off for Gold Dust.

The trio of belle dames slid to the ground every few yards. As usual there was a large flaw in Dick's plan. He'd forgotten to tell them to practice riding side-saddle. Bruised and battered, they finally got the hang of it, just as they were approaching town. They rode conspicuously in, making sure the inhabitants got a good view of the bogus No-Voice and his three floozies – a redhead, a blonde and a brunette; all thanks to the wigs they'd nicked from Tex's wardrobe. Having flashed themselves to all and sundry, they waited in a cool alleyway just across from the bank. Every five minutes or so, Dick brought out his enormous timepiece from the depths of his woolly poncho. He studied the hands as if he knew what he was looking at but unfortunately he'd never learned to tell the time! After three hours of waiting, they were getting a bit pissed off. Wilting there in the back passage that led from the main street, the three weirdos played 'Nag The Leader.' Dick was aghast at their bravery. Their women's rainments had given them the courage they'd lacked as men. He had no time to ponder on this, because around the corner thundered the money cart. The butch bandits leapt into action and watched from their safe hidehole the bogus routine, as the bank's employees carried out the money chest. Once it was on the cart, Dick's three 'lust maidens' sauntered across to the two big muscleboys.

'Well, hi there,' said Armless trying to peer out of a thick fringe of blonde wig, which had slipped almost to his nostrils.

The money guards got down from their buggy and walked openmouthed towards the nightmare vision. This was their undoing . . . Dick dashed around the back of them and kicked the drivers into the dirt. He leapt onto the cart, waited a few seconds for his fearless buddies to leap aboard too, and set off down the street with the spoils on wheels. They rode like women possessed down the main street, found they were going in the wrong direction and doubled back, running down the two guards as they went. By this time, most of the town had gathered on the sidewalks, craning their necks to see what was happening. Sheriff Rosen, ever in control of such situations, screamed for a posse. Four volunteers stepped forward. Chuck and Clit were there in a shot – they knew where their duty lay. Matthew wasn't far behind them, the good upstanding lad that he was. And Rose tagged along for the ride – it was ages since she'd been out on a horse. The other inhabitants of Gold Dust were very backward in coming forward. As usual, when help was needed, they melted away like butter in a hot frying pan. The shadow of Maddon still hung heavily over the township.

As the famous five prepared for the off, one of the guards raised his head from the dust and croaked:

'It was No-Voice that did it. He had three women helping him.'

Having delivered this valuable piece of information, the poor sod sank into unconsciousness; a nightmare of ponchos, cigars and ugly witches enveloped him. Doc Halliday rolled out of his surgery and staggered over to help the poor unfortunates.

The unbelieving five that made up the posse took a while to grasp what had been told them. Clit could not understand why No-Voice had turned to crime. He couldn't possibly need the money and why would he expose his womenfolk to such danger? It just didn't make sense. Of course, she and Rosen knew that the coffer was empty, but they had to go after No-Voice for attempted robbery and assault on the guards anyway. Confused, the five set off after the vanished vehicle. Three quarters of a mile out of Gold Dust, they came upon the abandoned buggy. The trunk had been broken into and was now empty. The thieves had scarpered with the contents. Clit laughed:

'Wait until they open those money pouches. I'd like to be there to see their faces.'

They looked around to see which direction the bandits had gone. It was then that the perspicacious Rose noticed that dear Sheriff Rosen was missing. Unbeknownst to them, he'd been knocked off his horse by a low-hung branch and was just then lying in agony back up the trail.

'He'll catch up,' said Chuck, ever-optimistic. And off the four roared, following the faint new tracks left by the robbers. They followed these as far as a stream, which lead into a lagoon in the foothills. It was here they found that they could go no further. The wily bandits had crossed the stream, but taken an indirect route through it. After hours of searching the opposite bank, the four fearless law people had to admit defeat. They had not a clue which way the escaping thieves had gone. They sat down under the shade of a clump of waterside trees to take stock of their situation. Little did they realise that their prey were doing the very same thing. Back at their hideout, Dick and his dastardly team, snorting and puffing with excitement, broke the seals and tipped the contents of the money bags into the dirt. To Dick's great chagrin, out fluttered not paper money but paper letters in a foreign language. French mostly!

The cool of the cottonwood trees refreshed the four pursuers. Clit lay with her head in Matthew's lap. Rose idly tickled Chuck's face with a piece of dried grass. Their horses stood nearby, tails flicking away the irritating evening flies.

Having given up on No-Voice for the moment, their thoughts turned to a more pressing problem – a method of getting rid of Jake Maddon. He had now redirected the water through the homesteaders' land, so Clit could not arrest him on that charge. They needed now to gather more evidence of the man's misdemeanours, in order that they could banish him from the vicinity. But nothing would come to their minds except sex.

'Geez,' thought Chuck, 'the water looks good.'

Without saying a word, he threw off his gunbelt and stepped out of his clothes. The others were treated to a flash of rounded white cheeks and then the water hid him from view. He shivered. It was almost as good a feeling as slipping his burning cock into Rose's refreshing cavern. Rose, who had become far less inhibited since her tiny adventure with Tex, followed him and was soon naked and frolicking in the cooling water. Chuck swam swiftly towards her, muscles coated with shiny rivulets of clear water. Rose felt him come up behind her and tweak a nipple hard. His cock, already granite-like, was banging clumsily around her bum. The ripples kept floating his sex raft off in the wrong direction. Bang, it was there again, bouncing against her buttocks. For a moment it felt like foe rather than friend – an enemy submarine trying to find its target. It came to rest between her bumflower and open water lily on the impenetrable tiny section of flesh between. Chuck's one-eyed bedsnake could not see under water, thought Rose. But she was wrong. The slippery eel wriggled and swivelled towards her snatch and was soon firmly embedded inside her. They heaved and splashed like a couple of playful porpoises.

On the bank, Clit and Matthew lay surrounded by scattered clothing. A naked, but still knickered Clit, curled around Matthew's bottom and happily pulled his dong from its pubic nest. Matthew had his hand behind him, with his fingers rammed down her knickers. He worked at her hot hairy hole, while she wanked him furiously. She felt herself coming but didn't want to waste herself on his finger; nor did she want to see his seed seep into the sand. They were desperate, both of them, and on the point of violent orgasms. There was no time to lose. Between them, they managed to lower the constricting knickers. Matthew could not resist the ripe moist plum that was suddenly in view. Drooling, he bent to Clit's winking beautiful beaver. He touched its outer portals with his tongue and Clit shuddered as the pink snake slid between her furry folds.

'No, no,' she gasped.

And taking hold of his head, she wrenched it out of her lap. Matthew got the message. He moved up her body and his cock shot like a plunger into her plughole. They came as soon as the dagger was buried up to the hilt in its sensuous scabbard.

The four lay in an untidy heap in that fuzzy sleepy sedated state that comes after orgasm. They dozed under the tree, listening to the soft gentle sounds of nature. A horse whinney brought them around. They sat up. Looking down the valley, they saw two Indians on white horses climbing the hill towards them. The four shag-happy people watched with interest as the aliens approached. The braves were obviously bent on a peaceful mission. The Indians reached them, jumped off their horses, bowed and sat down, crossing their legs as they did so. The four palefaces returned the compliment, only in the nude. It was a very strange scene indeed. As usual with Indians, they sat for a quarter of an hour in complete silence. At last, just as the four from Gold Dust were losing interest, the elder spoke.

'You don't know us, but we know you,' he said at Clit. 'Long time ago, you shot badman Black Sam, enemy of my people. We want peace not war. But Indians all fight soon unless beautiful young squaws – my daughters – return from town untouched. We give warning. Daughter return by badman Buster Brick or Indian make war.'

Then, bowing, they rose to their feet and disappeared down the hill. The last thing Clit and the others wanted was a war with the Indians.

'Who is this Buster Brick?' Clit demanded of the other three.

Only Chuck had heard of him: 'He came to town about six months ago. He's a big husky man with red hair; always has plenty of money. He bought a large wooden house just out of town on the Superstition side.

'If Brick has captured two young squaws, there will be heap bad trouble,' he added lapsing into the Indian vernacular.

Alarmed, the foursome dressed hurriedly and rode back to town without further heavy petting or orgasm. It was Rose's idea to stop at Ma O'Shea's. Ma kept a lodging house where the mailcoach drivers stayed and she knew all the news in town.

Ma's fat gossipy face creased into a frown at the mention of Buster Brick.

'I don't know nothing except this man has bought the big old house and he's doing it up. Making sixteen bedrooms they say. But what for, folks can't guess. I've been ill with the tuberculosis, 'cept I'd know more. But come back at suppertime. I've got my spies. We sure don't want no war 'cos some darn Easterner has captured two squaws.'

She nodded her head sagely and disappeared out the back.

Clit and Matthew returned later that evening. Chuck was unable to accompany them, as he'd developed a shocking headcold as a result of swimming in the bare. They found Lurex Tex sitting with Ma on the porch.

'Come here,' screeched Tex. 'I'll tell you all about that damn critter Buster Brick. He's sure up to no good.'

The story that came out made Clit and Matthew whistle with amazement. Apparently, Brick was about to start a new brothel to rival Tex's fun parlour. His rooms were done out in the latest, most luxurious flock wallpaper especially imported from Italy. He planned to open – although it was meant to be a secret – in about a month's time. Tex was near apoplexy. The best (or worst) was yet to come. His selling pitch was to offer eight young virgins on the opening night. These were, as everyone on Ma's porch knew, as rare as snow in the desert.

'Do something about it Clit,' pleaded the wretched Tex, 'or he will ruin me. *And* bring war. I don't know which is worse. You will find him living at Two Mile Ranch, four miles outside of Gold Dust. I'll help you in every way I can.'

Silence fell as four sets of grey cells worked like fury. The Marshall was the first to come up with anything bordering on an idea. She eyed Matthew up and down in the most peculiar manner. He backed away, not liking the look of her optics, one bit.

'Matthew,' she breathed, in her sweetest voice. The lad knew something bad was about to happen.

'You are perfect,' she oiled, 'for the part I have in mind. With your slight body . . .' Matthew made to interrupt but Clit swept on, 'and fair complexion, you could easily pass for a woman, if you wore lady's clothes and a heavy veil. You could pretend you'd hitched a lift on the mailcoach. Then, your next move would be to go out in all innocence to the Two Mile Ranch and say that you'd heard they let rooms. There, you take lodgings, saying that you're waiting to be joined by your father.'

Tex was overcome by the idea. She jabbed old Ma in the

ribs and promised to dress up Matthew the next day in her most discreet and smartest clothes. Ma could then drive him a mile or two out of town and join the mailcoach. Matthew, who, by this time, was so smitten with Clit, fell in with this idiotic plan.

'How am I going to speak?' he growled. 'They'll surely notice that my voice is a little strange.'

'Don't worry about that,' came in Tex. 'I've got just the thing. It was my great, great, great, great grandfather's truss.'

'I see,' said Matthew, comprehending the situation immediately.

Accordingly, at four o'clock the next afternoon, out of the mailcoach stepped a slim, heavily-veiled young lady, who, having been refused lodgings by Ma O'Shea, was sent in a buggy to the Two Mile Ranch. On arrival, Matthew, who was calling himself Miss Jane Sawyer, jumped down demurely from the cart and limped up to a passing cowhand. He asked if he knew whether he could have a room for a fortnight, until his father arrived. He replied in a surly voice that he had come to the wrong place. Matthew, unsure of his next move, found his heart beating unnaturally fast. A loud voice yelled at the ranch-hand to get to hell and a large red-haired fiery faced man in a large black hat asked Jane politely if he could be of any help. He explained his needs, in his new heavily-trussed voice. The man frowned for a moment and a doubtful look crossed his face. This was swiftly replaced by a sly cast of countenance.

'Well, ma'am,' he said, 'I don't make a habit of letting lodgings but I've never refused a young lady in distress yet. So, if you'll be prepared to put up with our simple fare and simple ways, then I guess I can put you up 'til your father arrives.'

Asking the 'girl' to wait there, he went indoors and came out in a couple of shakes with a scowling stout dark-haired woman. Without a word of welcome, this baggage seized Matthew's baggage and lugged it inside. The housekeeper ghoul showed the dragged-up Matthew to a room with a large four-poster bed. Four huge gilded mirrors hung on the walls. To one side was an ottoman covered with huge silk cushions and a little table with two chairs by it.

'Don't spoil it,' snapped the woman. 'Supper will be ready downstairs in an hour.'

She went out slamming the door in front of her. Matthew informed the woman that it was customary to close the door behind one. This she did, taking her leave of the confused lad. When Matthew, or rather Miss Jane, was alone, he changed into a long pale green gown with quite a bit of difficulty, unaccustomed as he was to fancy fiddlings. Outside his room, he heard the sound of doors opening and footsteps running downstairs. Taking his espionage work seriously, Matthew looked out of the door. Nobody was about and he decided to explore. His room was the first at the top of the stairs and beyond it lay a corridor with seven closed doors. Creeping on tip-toe, he tried one. It was locked. So were the others. At the last one, he heard a strange soft chanting. This super-sleuth had found the Indian girls, she/he/it had gone to rescue. Pressing his face to the door, Matthew whispered in his limited Indian dialect that they shouldn't worry, for help was at hand. He was sure he heard a sob of relief from within the locked room. Then Matthew went down to supper.

Buster Brick greeted Jane with a bow and apologised that supper was being taken in the drawing room. The workmen were still finishing the dining parlour, he informed her.

'Once that is finished, I will be able to open the fanciest guesthouse in the west.'

The guests at dinner comprised a pale beautiful girl of about eighteen, two young female Mexicans who spoke pigeon English, a lovely Irish girl with auburn hair and a young French girl with grey eyes and black hair. Last but not least, was a formidable fat Frenchwoman in a hideous green wig. Brick addressed her as Madame and she sat at the head of the table.

Surrounded by these tasty titbits of international femininity, Matthew discovered to his horror that his cock was rising in his skirts. Constricted as it was in the truss for raising his voice, it caused a great amount of pain. The diners were waited on by two Chinese boys, who moved silently about with the dishes. Matthew sat on the right hand of Buster Brick and soon realised that the houseowner did not believe Jane's story that she was being joined by her father. He asked the girl in the green dress, with a faint leer, how she had heard of his place. Deciding to try to win his sympathy, Jane said his mother had recently died and as his beauty (Matthew had the decency to blush) was the only asset he had, he'd decided to use it to make his way in the West. Brick replied:

'Well, you've come to the right place. But, by god, you're lucky. I only have room for eight wh . . . girls. Unfortunately I lost a young lady last week. She disobeyed an order and had the misfortune to be bitten by a rattler. But if you do what you are told, you will come to no harm and I will pay you well.'

A shiver ran down Matthew's falsies. After supper, Buster led him up to the Madame and told her that this was a wonderful new recruit to take poor dead Sophie's place. Madame shook him by the hand and told him that he only had a month to learn the secrets of Paris. In the morning, at nine o'clock sharp, he must attend lessons. In the middle of the night, Matthew crept along the corridor and whispered to the unknown Indian girls.

'Help is on it's way,' he hissed.

He returned to his room and fell into a deep and peaceful sleep. In the morning Madame gave him and the other girls, excluding the Indians who were obviously getting preferential treatment, their lessons.

'Now,' said the Madame. 'Never sleep with a man for pleasure – it is a waste of your body.' She directed this remark ironically at Matthew. 'Waste of frigging time,' he thought to himself, forgetting that he was a wolf in lady's clothing.

'If you have to, however, and slip up and sleep pleasurably with a man, you can still try to get something out of him.'

Turning to the others, she explained that her lesson that day dealt with muscular activity, as practised by the great French experts.

'Now, all tense your little cunts. Clench them.'

Our hero of the moment almost baulked at this command.

'Clench hard, and in the privacy of your own rooms you'll find candles in the cupboards by your beds. Insert them gently so's not to fracture your membranes – after all its most important that you're virgins – and practice squeezing as hard as you can. Many fortunes have been made by girls who've been able to develop a firm grip. It's greatest advantage, if you can achieve it, is if you can hold a man's cock so firmly, that he finds it impossible to ejaculate. This will always drive him insane with excitement. You can get anything out of a man so held and we're all in this for profit, dears. Now, please all go to your rooms and practice with the candles for one hour. If you need any assistance from me, I will be willing to give any help that I can.'

She leered as a parting shot: 'But remember not to insert them too far!'

Matthew went pale at the thought. The cheeks of his bum quivered involuntarily.

'Right girls, back in an hour.'

Just sixty minutes later, Matthew came back with his candle in a terrible state. Madame's next utterance caused him much alarm: 'I'm glad to say that Doc Halliday from town is going to attend you. He's going to be a consultant here at the brothel for the next two months. It is essential that the doctor examines you all before opening day in case,' and she gave a faint smile, 'any of you have cracked your maidenheads.'

The flesh on Matthew's cock crawled in his lace drawers. He had a faint suspicion he'd never pass the medical – even if he tucked it firmly in his pants.

'In a few moments, the doctor is going to come in and give a lecture on venereal diseases.'

'That'll be fun,' thought Matthew.

'. . . how you catch them and combat them. He will also give you knock-out pills to give any man you suspect of having a rotten knob. The first to be examined by the doctor will be Miss Jane Sawyer.'

Matthew's heart skipped a dozen beats at this news. But he went to see the doctor like the good girl he was.

The conservatory out back had been taken over by Halliday and his assorted bottles as a surgery. The place reeked of bad whisky and good ether. Matthew thought he might have a chance, as soon as he saw the medical man trying to get to his feet. After upward of five minutes, the aged doc managed to get his chin onto the consulting table and letched up at the feminine young thing that had just walked in. Pausing for a swig of his bottle and a sniff of his ether, he ordered the confused Matthew to take his clothes off.

Feigning modesty, Matthew hung his head and blushed. Doc's pink watery eyes stared balefully at him.

'Alright, alright, dear, go behind the screen and undress. I won't look; I'll just feel.'

With a sigh of relief, Matthew scuttled, skirts trailing, behind the bamboo partition. He quickly stripped, flinging his outer garments over the screen as he'd seen them do in the magic lantern shows. He was down to his coms, when a gnarled, blue-veined hand crept stealthily around into his airspace.

'Tits,' intoned the inebriate medic. 'Give us yer tits.'

Matthew glanced around in panic; but in the nick of time, happened upon a miniature orange tree soaking up the sunshine in the conservatory. He plucked two of the biggest offerings from the branches and shoved them into the waiting palms.

'Small but firm,' screamed the drunkard. 'Pubes,' he shouted dictatorially.

Matthew, in an effort not to be outdone or undone by this

fool, reached behind him and grasped his cock firmly between his legs, pulling it into the crease of his arse. The doctor's hand, he guided to his now flat unencumbered hairy area. Halliday felt around and patted the pretend pussy.

'That's OK,' he cackled. 'Now, let's have a feel at yer doodah.'

Terror crept from Matthew's toenails to the nape of his neck. He thought it was all over; he felt sure his number was up. 'Keep calm,' he told himself. His optics did a frantic swivel in his head. It was the plum tree that saved his bacon. He grabbed a fruit from the tree and, with sweating fingers, peeled it rapidly. He dug the stone out with a thumb and presented the split offering to the drunken old fool. He placed the fruit in situ to make the subterfuge a little more believable. The doc inserted a black-nailed forefinger and exclaimed with glee: 'Juicy, for sure. And tight as a tiny plum.' He added this unwittingly, hitting the nail securely on the head.

'OK, get dressed, you randy little cow,' he barked.

Matthew didn't need to be told twice and, as he left the conservatory, the doc was scribbling on his desk pad. It looked as if he was through this medical hurdle. But the worst was yet to come.

The following day, Madame gave them all a lesson on oral lovc-making.

She lectured: 'A mouth is not only for speaking, and teeth not only for chewing food. Nor is the tongue only for tasting. All three can be used to great effect in the sex game.'

She produced a wooden model of a penis and showed the girls how to suck it. Needless to say, Matthew did not take like a duck to water to this cock-sucking. It was not something he'd ever thought he'd have to do. But he pretended it was one of Clit's nipples and this inner knowledge got him through the ordeal.

Madame went on to show them how to run their lips up and down the veins on its lower half and how to gently bite and pull at it with their teeth. Then she produced six cocks made of sugar and told the girls to take them to their rooms and yet again practice their craft – licking and sucking.

She added: 'I've always found it a good idea to train girls to fellate on sugar cocks. Then, when a girl is faced for the first time with a real cock, she is able to shut her eyes and pretend to herself that what she is sucking is just candy. Pretence is very valuable in love-making. But one word of advice – never agree to suck a man's prick without first appearing horrified. Secondly, only do it for a substantial present.'

Matthew thought to himself that it would have to be a *very* substantial present to get him to do it.

'. . . and thirdly, always tell him he is the only man to whom you have done such a thing.'

She concluded with a little dietary advice: 'Be careful in slobbering over your sugar cocks. Don't break them and don't bite them hard, because men don't like that.'

Matthew nodded feverishly in agreement.

'They are excellent training material but don't eat them all up, for it will make you fat and spoil your lunch!'

What interested Matthew was why the Indian girls were kept apart from the others. True, they could not understand English, but you don't have to speak English to lick a gingerbread old man! He decided to make up to Buster Brick – as a woman – so, at lunch that day he whispered to him as he was eating a potato, that he could not wait until he lost her virginity and then could go to bed with him.

Buster almost choked on his calorie intake. His eyes dilated with lust and he reached for Matthew's hand under the table. What he grabbed was long and hot, but it wasn't Matthew's hand . . . He was too delirious in his love to notice though. Fluttering his false lashes, Matthew asked Buster to take him for a walk that afternoon. After lunch, the unlikely pair left the ranch. Matthew took the man's arm and mentioned how strong he thought Buster was. He was getting well into character here.

Turning the subject from strength, Matthew went on: 'You know Buster, I have not told you the complete truth.

My father is not coming out here at all. I don't even know who he is.'

Pa Webster, if he *had* been dead, would have turned over in his grave at this remark.

'My mother keeps a brothel in Pepper Steak City and wants me to take over in five or six years time. She said that, in the great American tradition, in order to know the ropes, or dicks in this case I suppose, I must start right at the bottom and work my way down. When she heard a real fancy house was to be opened up here, she sent me along. I hope you're not shocked.'

'Take a lot more than that to shock me, youngster,' said Buster curtly. 'I can't wait to get my hot cock between your thighs.'

This was quite explicit enough for Matthew to grasp Buster's meaning and he suddenly wished he hadn't been so bold.

Undaunted, Matthew got bolder and began telling Buster his own business. Well-briefed by Tex on the subject – she in fact had given him a handbook on brothels for this express purpose – Matthew poked a doubtful finger at Buster's schemes. He accused the brothel-owner of not providing for weirdos, who his mom said pay best. He went on, as Jane, to say that his mother kept girls specifically for those who liked a touch of the whip, and those who liked a clank of the chains too. Those who wore high-heels and trod men into the ground shouldn't be overlooked either.

He ended casually: 'We also provide some girls who scream and yell and fight as if they hate every minute of it. The more they cry, the more the fellas like it. But perhaps you are not so sophisticated out here,' he ended bitchily.

Buster rose like a fish to a fly: 'Look Jane,' he replied. 'Don't get any ideas that I'm dumb or you'll regret it for the rest of your life. Jeez, I know all about every scene going. As a matter of fact,' he said conspiratorially, 'I've got two Indian girls who yell if anyone goes anywhere near them. Mary, the housekeeper, can't go to feed them without a whip.'

'Oh, you are clever, Bust, you think of everything,' said Matthew, pressing his hand to Buster's fly in a simulated show of affection.

Coincidentally, the next day, Madame gave instruction in sadism and told the pupils that they must not be surprised if the toughest wanted to dress up in girl's clothes and be soundly birched. They were instructed never to show surprise, always to say that every variation was possible – only, it cost more money. After the lesson was over, Matthew went and asked Buster Brick if he would send her into town that afternoon, as Madame had so excited his other ego with the flagellation lesson, that he wanted to buy himself a whip. Then he burst into more conversation:

'Oh, Buster, could I look after the Indians on Mary's day-off tomorrow and whip them if they're naughty.'

'Gee,' said Buster, 'you sure are a sexy bitch. But I guess you can give them a tanning if it takes your fancy. But look out when you bed me – I won't want no whipping. Get that straight.'

Directly Matthew got into town, he bought a leather bull whip. The storekeeper told him proudly. 'Cuts like a knife that one.'

Taking care he was not followed from the grocer's with a little sex counter, he hurried around to Ma O'Shea's. She quickly summoned Clit. Matthew told them all his news, omitting strangely the suck-a-dick episode; but adding: 'I've thought of how we can kill two vaginas with one cock – destroy Tex's competition and rescue the squaws.'

'How?' chorused Ma and Clit.

'Well, first I need a decoy – female, of course. Someone's daughter or wife. Someone, who if the relative were really threatened, would charge to their rescue.'

'How about Sheriff Rosen's daughter,' injected Ma O'Shea. 'That girl, Myrtle, goes for a walk every night,' she said, nudging the others. 'The sheriff thinks it's a harmless evening pastime but the whole town 'cept him knows different. She has her arse screwed off every night by Granville

Goodnight behind his gunstore. They say,' said Ma O'Shea, warming to her story, 'that he puts everything but a rifle butt into her.'

'Great,' said Matthew, 'while she is flat on her back or any other bizarre position she may be in on Thursday, you can hurl a note-wrapped stone through the sheriff's window. This should say that his daughter is being held prisoner at Two Mile Ranch. Leave the rest to *moi* . . .'

The others surveyed him strangely at this Gallic outburst.

Matthew, seeing their astounded looks, apologised, explaining that a bit of the Madame must have rubbed off on him already!

Wednesday was Mary's day off. She always visited her aged parents on this, her free, day. Matthew, with his whip at the ready, visited the two captive Indian girls at lunchtime. He found each of them chained to a narrow wooden bed. One of them sported a nasty weal on her pretty face – obviously the result of Mary's over-zealousness with the whip. Matthew whispered to them in the dialect he'd learnt from his pa but they cowered in terror. He told them, as best he could, that the next evening, when they heard the sound of raised voices below, they should scream at the top of their voices . . . and go on screaming until help arrived. 'Practice now,' he said to each in turn, and they gave forth blood-curdling yells.

Downstairs, Buster smiled and said to Madame with satisfaction: 'That broad is a hot number indeed.'

On Thursday morning, Madame gave a repeat lesson in cock-sucking, followed by vaginal exercises. The pupils all yawned with the repetitiveness of it all! Again Matthew, as Jane, asked Buster to take him for a stroll around the patch of land surrounding the ranch-house. As sundown approached, Matthew appeared nervous. But meanwhile, in town, all was going well. At 7 o'clock on the dot, Sheriff Rosen was sitting at his desk in his office. He had his legs on the top of the piece of furniture and a glass of liquor in his hand. A large stone crashed through the window. His first reaction was to shoot whoever had so rudely disturbed him; his second to read the paper wrapped around the missile. It read:

'Come quick to Two Mile Ranch. Your daughter is a prisoner.' It was signed 'A Friend.'

'What a bloody *chutzpah*, my life,' he said.

Jumping to his feet, he strapped on his weapon. 'Hey, boys,' he yelled to a bunch of ugly-looking thugs who were standing grouped outside his office, waiting for such a disaster to occur: 'Three of you saddle your horses and follow me. Someone is holding my Myrtle at Two Mile Ranch.'

'Some people will hold anything,' thought the men.

Two minutes later, the yiddish sheriff and his gentile posse were galloping at full speed in the vague direction of the ranch brothel. Meanwhile, at Two Mile Ranch, all was peaceful, all was calm. It was a scene of domestic bliss. The girls were preparing dinner, and the cowboys feeding their horses. Buster and Madame were playing strip-poker in the *salon du thé*. Buster was winning hands down, Madame's udders being already exposed to view.

Their calm was broken by a tremendous commotion outside as the sheriff and his men arrived in the yard. They rode their horses straight into the house, dismounted, and strode into the salon. Buster leapt to his feet, while Madame tried to cover her nakedness with a jack and a king.

'Why sheriff. . .' smarmed Buster.

But he was cut off in mid-smirk. 'Where's Myrtle?' shouted Rosen.

'Myrtle?' repeated Buster dumbfounded. 'I don't . . .'

His further pathetic protestations were drowned by the caterwauling which echoed through the house.

'Goddam you, boy,' yelled the sheriff, 'they're killing Myrtle.'

Meanwhile Myrtle was flat on her back receiving all the prick she could gobble. As Granville Goodnight came, Buster went. Went out like a light, that is, from a punch, the like of which the sheriff had never dished out before. He blazed upstairs and, following the screams of anguish, came to the locked door. He pumped bullets through the keyhole in no uncertain manner and bust in to find no Myrtle, but two screaming squaws instead. One hour later, Buster handcuffed and with a snout like a mashed beetroot, was still being questioned by the officer of the law. Clit rode in to say that Myrtle had returned. She had just gone for her usual scr . . . stroll!

'Lucky for you, Buster,' said Rosen, 'but you ain't got out of hot water yet. If them Indians feel they have lost face, they'll make sure their braves roast your goollies around their campfire. They must have their revenge some how.'

It was then that Clit interfered with the sheriff. 'I know what to do,' she said. 'Boys,' she aimed at the posse, 'strip Buster and tie him to the bed. And you girl,' poking Matthew in the ribs, 'finish undressing Madame there and lash her to another. We will let the Indians whip them and that will satisfy their pride.'

In ten seconds flat, Buster and Madame were bound to two beds, side by side. The Indian girls were brought into the room. When they understood what they were going to be allowed to do, they chatted to each other with squeaks of delight. They were to give ten strokes each to the wicked kidnappers. The first girl took Matthew's new whip in her hand and struck hard and swiftly. Each blow fell in exactly the same place. The second squaw was equally accurate on the other victim. Buster, in all this, tried to restrain his cries but Madame yelled and screamed and begged for mercy.

To no avail . . .

Clit then sorted out the situation: 'Unless you pay each of these squaws 500 dollars, Buster, we will let them skin your totem pole.'

In a furious rage, Buster agreed. The thrilled Indians were sent back to their tribe, three mountains distant. The whores, terrified, packed their bags and moved off to more prickly pastures. This left Buster and Madame to dine together and cry together. Miss Jane Sawyer drove sedately into town and was last seen entering Ma O'Shea's house with Clit. A couple of hours later, Matthew, manhood restored by the Marshall, was seen to jump on his horse and ride thoughtfully home. Miss Jane Sawyer was never seen again.

Chapter Twelve

THE BIG BELCH CONNECTION

Meanwhile, Jake Maddon was sitting with a group of friends in Tex's bar. He was giving his final instructions.

'Have you buggers got it clear? She has got to be put out of the way once and for all. She is a continuing pain in my arse. But do it slowly. We don't want her to die quick. She deserves more than that. Make sure she relishes every moment of her untimely demise,' he said smacking his evil lips together.

'Be back here at midnight.'

He slammed down his empty glass. The boys, Huck, Red and Jed, rose to their feet as a man and strode out of the bar. As they rode out of town, Jed said over his shoulder: 'We'll make her suffer, we sure will.' He gave a high-pitch falsetto laugh, which seemed strange issuing forth from his luxuriant black moustache. But Red did not laugh. A small sandy haired man, his little pink eyes were always darting around his head with fear. 'I think there ought to be more of us. Marshall Clit Westwood might have friends with her. She usually does. And then we'll be outnumbered.'

'Shut your bloody trap,' said Huck. 'We know she's going to Webster's for a leg-over. Who takes their friends fucking? We'll bushwhack her in Big Belch, string a rope across the track and see if she enjoys her fuck, flying through the air!'

The three rode on laughing.

They knew Clit had her randy rendezvous with Matthew at ten o'clock. Once they'd reached the Big Belch, they made a careful examination of the ground and tethered their horses near Webster's end. They set their ambush at a narrow point, where the track ran between two huge cock-shaped cacti.

Fixing a rope around one they laid it lax across the trail and covered it in dust. As Clit rode by at a gallop, they would jerk it up and, if she survived the fall, the fun would then begin. It took them ten minutes to get the rope ready and then the three hoodlums sat and waited. Just then, Clit was preparing for her ride to her lover; not only to fuck Matthew, but to collect her private mail from their farm too. This came once a week by Wells Fargo. She did this, as she was sure that one of Jake Maddon's spies would steam open her privates if she let them. Jake's spies were everywhere. However, her regular visits had been interpreted in the worst . . . or the best . . . sense. Local opinion had it that she fucked Matthew every Monday. This was true. And, for once, Clit was grateful to the gossips.

She was about a mile from Big Belch, when she pulled up Brasso, sharp. A coyote, with a pup behind, had crossed the track up ahead at a rare old speed. Clit sat still while Brasso trembled and pulled at his bit.

'Why,' Clit asked herself,' did the coyote cross the road? There is only scrub, desert and Big Belch between here and the Webster's farm,' she mused further. She wondered what sort of fright the shy beast had experienced, to make it bolt up this by-pass. She thought carefully. 'Ah, ah,' she said aloud. If somebody was hiding up ahead of her, Big Belch was the perfect place for a bushwhack. A thin smile moved across her lips. She'd ride around the Belch and come up in a surprise hiccup attack. If anybody was waiting, well, they would get a bit of a shock seeing her riding like wind up their bums the wrong way. She touched Brasso with her polished spurs. Everything about this lady shone. She galloped off to avoid a massacre. One hour later – it was a very long way around – she tethered Brasso to a steel-wool wall west of the Belch. She took cover amongst the dusty rocks and crept slowly along in the increasing gloom. Shortly, she came across the sound of voices. Clit edged forward until she was only a few yards from the unsuspecting men. Jed was saying in his angry falsetto voice:

'I just can't wait any longer. If she doesn't come soon, she'll certainly pay for keeping us waiting.'

'Hush,' replied Huck, 'a voice travels far in this silence. I only hope she's coming. She *is* coming. But by my reckoning she's an hour late.'

Silence reigned down. Then Huck said: 'Jed, go and see if those ants are hungry.'

Jed, carrying a lantern, blundered within two yards of Clit but didn't even catch a whiff of her. Or Brasso. He returned within minutes. 'Jesus Christ,' he said, 'they are mad. I guess when we stake that hussy down on them, they'll have a real feast.'

Clit took a quick breath. The bastards! Jake's henchmen, were planning to tie her to a mentally-disturbed ant-nest – the most agonising death in the West. She must be careful. One mistake and it would be ants up her pants. The three men had clustered around two shaded lanterns. But even as she watched, Jed rose and said: 'I'll guess I'll pee.'

'I guess I'll join you,' said the other two. A lot of guessing and a lot of peeing went on. Clit, sensing her moment had come, moved out from the shadow of the rock and found herself facing a row of urinating penises.

'Reach,' she said brandishing her two six-shooters.

The men froze. Three jets of pee provided the only movement. Then Red reached for his gun; so quickly that he actually had it out of his holster before Clit's bullet smashed his hand.

'Reach,' she said again quietly. Huck and Jed slowly obeyed while Red moaned and clasped his fingers.

'Keep 'em up, Red,' said Clit. 'Unless you'd like your other hand mashed.

Bellowing, he did as he was told. The three thugs stood, hands elevated, cocks sticking out of their trousers, looking ridiculous, with waterfalls of wee soaking into their chaps. Clit came out into the open.

'So, you were aiming to feed me to the ants were you? I guess I don't want to disappoint them. As you've promised them a meal, they shall have one. Lead on to the ant's nest, Jed.'

Picking up a lantern, she followed. Jed cried out as he walked: 'I've suddenly remembered that I've forgotten where it is.'

'Perhaps this will remind you,' said Clit as she shot off his hat.

It did, and in a moment they were upon the insect home. A huge anthill had been overturned and beside it lay a rope and four pegs.

'Now you go and stand by it or I'll kill you stone dead – and you can't get deader than that.'

Mumbling into their hairpieces, they obeyed. Clit went and sat down, after placing the lantern, so that she was in the shadows. The light shone on their sweating faces. She tossed Jed her knife and told him to cut the other men's clothes off. Silently, he hacked at their boots and belts, throwing their guns and his own safely to her. Soon the trio were stark naked.

Then she ordered Huck: 'As the leader of this trio I'm going to extend you the compliment of being the first to get ants up your arse. You can go and sit on the nest for five minutes and if you get off the nest before I say, I'll blow your balls from your body. Understand?'

Huck understood and sat down. At once, the ants bit into his soft parts. He yelled as they crawled up his crotch. Three times he started to get off his hotbed. Each time a bullet reminded him to get back.

Mad with rage and pain, he stayed put. At the end of five minutes, it was Jed's turn. He flung himself on his knees and begged for mercy. But the iron-faced Clit would not be swayed. For five of the longest minutes of his life, he had to be ants' fodder. Then, Clit gave Red to the rapacious creepy-crawlies. After they'd all had a turn at musical-ants, Clit threw Red a pair of handcuffs and made him fasten Jed and Huck together. Collecting all their belongings under her arm, she wished them goodnight.

'Hey,' shouted Huck, 'you can't leave us here. We'll never get home to our supper.'

'That's your business,' Clit replied. 'Sleep well.'

With that, she strode off, leaving Red nursing his shot hand and the other imbeciles naked and cuffed together. She soon found their three mounts and tethered them in a line to her own. She felt sure that she had time to ride quickly to Matthew's for her mail and a sliver of steel, before returning to town to deal once and for all with big JM. Now she had the rope with which to hang him. The evidence she needed . . .

Matthew kicked out the embers of the fire and walked across to where Clit was lying and staring at the stars. Clit had hot-horsed to the Webster's ranch and had found her young lover at work outside. He had been branding the family's one cow – hence the fire. Now, he slid under the blanket beside her with his boots still on and, without any more ado, lifted her skirt above her belly exposing the lot. She stiffened and so did he. Her body woke to the nearness of him. He rubbed her small flat stomach for a time, looking deeply into her eyes all the while. She trembled with anticipation. The sound of rough breathing was in her ears. The feel of rough hands was on her breasts. The aching that started somewhere deep inside turned into a fiery sweet pain in her loins. She felt it now so strongly, as Matthew's hands roamed and long fingers caressed and probed. They moved over her nipples and then down over her trembling thighs, gently circling the place where the ache was. And, oh, what a bitter sweet sensation this was! She moaned and twisted beneath him, as he fumbled with his fly to let his beast out of its serge cage. The head nuzzled for a moment up against her furry mound; then, at a stroke, buried itself deep inside. She gasped as he delved into her dunking pot. He paused in his pumping and she felt his fingers stretching the walls of her quim. One, two, three fingers forced entry, joining the joint already up her lovecave. Her cries filled the empty night. Then, in the stillness that followed, a confused coyote answered back. His boots and leathers were rough on her thighs, as he began a new onslaught. She did not want him to stop, though, or take his fingers from her warmed pleasure pot. Nor did she want the mammoth erection to slip from her. She was enjoying it far too much. Her thighs loosened and parted even wider in welcome to the monstrous tool. Her legs kicked the blanket from them and waved palely in the moonlight, like the tendrils of some exotic flora. His hands were now beneath her, lifting and separating her cheeks. His lips on hers, explored the sensuous delights of her mouth. Her moans mingled with his breath. His chest and lips smothered her panting cries and then he, himself, let out a great bellow of satisfaction. Wrapping her legs tightly around his thrusting buttocks, she swam in and out of her floating ecstacy. He convulsed and flooded her with his come. The muscles inside her rippled up and down his spewing shaft. She was in a sexual puddle, drowning in her own wave-after-wave of pleasure. Like a pool when a stone is dropped in the water. Never-ending. His weight pressed her into the hard earth. She could not move. And then the fullness within her fell away, as he rolled off panting.

With Matthew's sighs of 'I love you,' ringing in her ears, Clit sped off to complete the rest of her night's work. As the clock in Tex's bar struck twelve, Jake Maddon glanced at the swing doors with a keen look of anticipation on his face. He brought out his gold repeater and looked at its bejewelled hands.

'A bottle of rye for Huck, Red and Jed,' he called to Abe, the bartender. Abe placed a bottle and four glasses on a brass tray and carried it across the crowded room. He was just about to put it on Jake's table, when the swing doors flashed open to reveal, none other than, Clit with a six-shooter in each hand. Jake froze in his knickers, a glass of liquor half way to his lips. Clit walked briskly across the saloon. All eyes were upon her. Except for an occasional crossed optic, that is! She sat down opposite Jake.

'Are you going to offer me some of this rye?' she asked

politely, pointing to the bottle and four glasses. Abe melted away into the background.

'After all,' continued Clit, 'you seem to be expecting friends. Won't I do instead?'

Jake gave an uneasy laugh, which sounded remarkably like a child's rattle.

'Why sure, help yourself,' he said, covering as best he could.

'I'm going to,' said Clit pouring out two fingers of the honey-coloured liquor. At the same time, she put her other hand, which still held a six-shooter, onto the table and pointed the gun straight at Jake's heart. You could have heard a splatter of sperm drop. In fact, it was said afterwards, the only sound was that of sweat dropping from Jake's forehead to the wooden table top.

Clit relaxed in her chair and savoured the moment. She wriggled around, positioning her boobs provocatively in front of the perspiring outlaw.

'Are you sitting comfortably,' she began. 'I have an interesting story to tell you. Tonight, I was about to pass through Big Belch on Brasso when an animal gave me a warning of danger ahead. Smelling trouble, I rode in a circle, ignoring the direct route. Doubling back on my tracks, I found your miserable posse of pansies – Huck, Jed and Red – hiding in a cleft. They were waiting for me with a trip-rope, an ants nest and ropes and stakes. It was a jolly party on an ants hill that they had in mind. I had a friendly talk with them, though, during which poor Red had the misfortune to have one of his hands severed from its arm. They've all got ant-nibbled naughties too. So, as they couldn't make it, I'm here to have a drink with you instead. Isn't that nice?' she added, winking at the stupefied jerk.

'I can't say you look very pleased about it,' she reproached him. Abruptly she stopped being sociable, and turned on Jake. Nudging him in the ribs with the cold steel of the sharp-shooter, she indicated he was to get to his feet.

'Now step outside the door,' she barked, 'take off your

clothes and hurry.' She squeezed off a shot, which whizzed through his bow legs. Jake didn't waste time – he was no fool – and while he was about it, Clit snatched his gold repeater, threw the piece in the air and blew the valuable watch to pieces with one single shot. She turned her deadly charms and the guns back to Jake. She gave him a shove through the swing doors back into the joint. He bounced, like a roulette ball when it hits the studs on the wheel, as he came into contact with the floor. His look of terror gave him away. He was sure his number was up and it certainly wasn't a lucky one.

'Get an erection!' she ordered.

This was worse than Jake feared. Leering faces sniggered over the top of every available piece of cover in the room.

'Go on, pull it,' Clit went on.

Blushing, Jake fumbled with his flopping sausage. It floundered around like a flabby fish out of water. It had no life in it at all.

'Get one of his favourite whores,' yelled Clit to the barman. Abe scuttled away like a frightened rabbit and came back bearing a hearty-faced big girl called Scarlet. Clit whispered in the girl's ear and a broad grin spread across her face. She reached out and gave Jake's cock a few swift strokes. Soon, it was protruding like a hatpeg from his bush. The huge crowd of drunken men let out a cheer as she bent to take the bulbous weapon in her mouth. Jake shoved up hard, unthinking in his frustration and rage, and nearly choked poor Scarlet. She bit into the fleshy rod, enough to let him know that she had all the aces in this particular game. The joker was between her teeth. She nibbled at the tip of it, then covering the head with her mouth, let it slide full-length down her throat. It went down until her muscles spasmed. She gagged and withdrew. With finger and thumb, she briskly trigged the pole, until it swelled dangerously and threatened to spill its load prematurely. She tried to calm it with a kiss, but only exacerbated the situation. Jake, overcome by the events of the last few moments of his public shame, came in great frightening jerks. He stood in the puddle of his own humiliation to hear Clit saying the unbelievable words:

'Now, get down on your knees, you bastard, and rub your nose in it.'

Jake hesitated. This was another of his mistakes. He felt the force of Clit's metal-tip boot ram up the crack of his arse. He spreadeagled, his nose skidding through his pool of come. His face followed with a splat. But, even then, his degredation was not over. Clit had another ace up her sleeve. She commanded Abe to fetch some rope. Then, with the barman's help, she tied the hapless Jake to one of the saloon's swing doors. There he stayed all night, rocking aimlessly back and forth, as people came into the tavern.

Now that Mr. Big had been tamed by the ruthless marshall, everyone in town came to poke fun at him. Their bravado was surprising, as they flipped him back and forth on his door prison. Because of the antagonism shown towards Maddon, Clit felt safe to leave him there unguarded for the rest of the night. She made her first big mistake . . . She'd underestimated the two-facedness of the townspeople. Jake's supporters were thick on the ground. When she came to collect her prize the following morning, to jail him for attempted murder by ants, she found cut ropes dangling from the door, which was still warm, like the lavatory seat, too. The bird had flown. He'd Biggsed it!

Chapter Thirteen

NO-VOICE MEETS HIS ALTERED EGO

Meanwhile back at the ranch, very little was happening. But out at Jake Maddon's place, things were frenzied. The boss-man, to his troops surprise, had arrived back at home naked and spent. He'd had enough. He told his hands that he was leaving Gold Dust for good. Clit had literally beaten him into the ground. It was more than a man could stand. He could no longer walk the street with his cock held high, making people quake with fear as his boots hit the dirt. He packed a few of his most priceless belongings into tasteful matching saddlebags, got dressed and rode off as fast as his horse would take him away. He'd been riding all night – and had crossed the International Date Line – when he heard the warning gunshot way behind him. He looked over his shoulder and nearly fell off his horse at what he saw. Firing her gun in the air, blonde hair streaming behind her, was a girl rider. Her bodice was torn open and her boobs exposed to the prairie dust. Since it wasn't in his nature to fear no female ('cept the cantankerous Clit), Jake reigned in and turned his horse to face her. She was a pretty thing, in spite of the dirt on her face and the flapping blouse with its torn buttons. Her duflops bounced like lush melons, though streaked in grime. The badman sucked in his breath and waited for the female rider to come up alongside.

'Mister,' she gasped, stuffing her gun back in its holster, 'Please help me.'

Jake fixed his eyes on her tits.

'Please, mister, I'm in a heap of trouble and need help.'

Jake shoved a cigar butt in his mouth and eyed her with a look of suspicion and animal lust. It briefly crossed, what was left of his post-Clit mind, that she could easily be a trap sent by the devious marshall. Jake sniffed.

'Well, I'll be darned,' he thought. 'Despite her bedraggled appearance, she smells as sweet as orange blossom.'

'What are you doing out here?' he chewed on his cigar.

'My mama and papa's been murdered by the Indians and they raped me too. All of them – the whole tribe.'

Jake didn't wholly believe this boastful tale. The Indians had been quiet for months; since they attacked the Wild Wild West wagon train, anyway. He hadn't known them do any raping or looting since last fall!

The girl climbed down from her horse, holding the end of her torn bodice together with one hand. Jake jumped down beside her and took her horse's reins and tethered them to the branch of a conveniently-placed tree. His next move was almost a reflex action for the sex-mad villain. He simply reached out for the girl grabbing her arm, pulled her to him completely ignoring her cries of alarm. With one casual movement, he ripped her shirt from her. He grabbed her tits in his giant paws and leered into her face. She lowered her eyes despairingly and pleaded as if to herself:

'No, please, not again.'

But Jake, in moments like this, was a man of iron resolve. Grunting like an overweight bull, he fumbled with the girl's belt and then yanked her trousers down around her ankles. Seeing he meant business, she changed tack and obligingly stepped out of them. She lay down on the pile of garments now on the floor. She spread her legs wide, knees in the air and feet off the ground. Her moist pink slot gaped wide and Jake, freeing himself from the confines of his own coms, fell on top of her like an epileptic elephant. The girl had grown quiet and strangely subdued, as the monster heaved and slobbered above her. Her eyes shone with pleasure at every poke. She flexed her muscles professionally and curled her legs around his back, arching up to meet his short stabbing jibes. Jake had done a lot of fucking in his time, some of it without consent. However, even he began to detect a subtle difference in the piece of ass manipulating his member so adroitly. The jaw-like wall of muscle in her slippery tunnel of love gripped his length in a manner he had not experienced before. Not in all his years of banging . . . This was something he mused as he thumped away. And then, as her hand reached behind his thighs to reach for his balls, he steamed up like a locomotive for the final pant. He quickened his pace and laboured above her. In a moment it was over; his spunk jetting up to the neck of her womb like squirts from a water pistol. The girl beneath him yelped for joy and tightened the grip around him with her flexing legs. Her cunt tightened, circling his now-flaccid tool; swallowing it and milking it with practised undulations. Despite himself, Jake felt it coming to life again. It rose up like the Loch Ness Monster, stretching the wet walls of her cunt to bursting. He banged slowly at first, then went faster, amid slapping noises like wet fish upon a plate. Later, after nightfall, the laboured breathing of the rapacious Jake could be heard coming from a small clearing in the middle of a clump of cottonwood trees. It was only in the grey dawn on the following day when he'd plugged her eighty four times in all and delivered the very last dribble from his aching balls, that silence settled on the prairie at long last. When he awoke from a much-needed reviving sleep, it was to find, with no little surprise, that he was tied face down, bare bum in the air, to his horse. No-Voice was leaning against a tree smoking a cigar and watching Jake from under the huge brim of his sombrero. The hunter mounted Silvo, brother of Brasso, and sister of Silver Dip, tethered the leading rein of Jake's mount to his saddle and, without a backwards glance, cantered away.

Jake felt like a cock out of cunt. Again, he had been duped into a position of no-power. Clit had come along and rubbed his nose in the dirt and more. Then, the beautiful, supposedly-distressed young waif had happened by, and taken him in. Mind you, the hours and hours of fucking, he had enjoyed! But it didn't make his present position any the easier to endure. He was bare-arsed, hog-tied over his critter and it looked like he was heading into town and into jail, fast.

Then, a remarkable thing happened to baddie Maddon. He had an idea! Suppose, he thought, that No-Voice didn't know he, No-Voice was wanted by the forces of good for bank robbery. Suppose he didn't realise that Wanted posters had gone up all over town for him. No-Voice seemed to be taking an easy ride into town with him. And poor unfortunate No-Voice would get his come-uppance, once they rode up that main street. Maddon would have to keep the grin off his face, or the wily hunter would suspect. Had the man taken leave of his senses? Surely he wasn't going to ride into town as bold as Brasso on his Silvo? He couldn't be so stupid as to think nobody had seen him bungle the bank raid. But this is how it appeared at the moment. Poor Maddon's grey cells just couldn't fathom it out.

He would hazard a question at his captor. Trying to conceal his large smirk, he cricked his neck around to face the arse-end of No-Voice's horse. He launched into his somewhat tactless line of questioning:

'How much money did you find in the chest that you stole from the bank?'

Tactless wasn't the word . . .

'The whole of Gold Dust knew what the contents of the case actually was. He, he, he. I hear it was full of foreign correspondence. Were they Welsh with leaks in? Or Dutch with clogs on so you could hear yourself coming?'

No-Voice seemed to be baffled by Jake's jokey babblings. After all, he was hardly in a position to crack jokes – if indeed that was what he might call them. He resolved to find out what the fuck Maddon was talking about. He found this needling was getting under his skin. What was the goon gabbing about? He whipped his horse around so that he was facing the unpleasant bundle strapped to the palamino behind him. He placed his handmade boot under the ruffian's chin and glared at Maddon.

A hefty blow to the head dulled Maddon's senses. He got the silent message and managed to form a reply in his throat.

He decided that truth would out and he might just as well gab the gab before his neck was broken.

'Well, you know what I mean. You robbed that bank payroll. You were seen by the whole town. You were with your floozies and you ran over a guard. You pulverised him into the ground and they don't know yet whether he'll live or die. And if Doc Halliday attends him, he'll probably die.' He raved on feverishly.

'You're the most wanted man this side of Ketchup,' he added for effect. 'A posse of at least four was on your trail until they got waylaid by their nasty sexual habits. Fuck-a-duck. Are you a complete imbecile in poncho and sombrero?' His questions lapsed into the Mexicano.

No-Voice, whacking him with his sombrero (joining in with the Mexican carnival atmosphere), shrugged his shoulders at the lunatic's ravings.

'This is just Maddon's way of tricking me out of my milk-coated coconut bar,' thought No-Voice when he'd assessed the situation. He turned his horse back on its way – in the direction of the town – and completely ignored the hot air which continued to geyser out of Maddon's hole.

He was riding quite happily, then, thinking of how he'd spend all of Maddon's bounty on fine dresses for the girls in his life. Another sombrero broke into his reverie and crept over the crest of the hill in front of him. It was followed by a cigar, poncho and Silvo's twin. Even No-Voice's cool slipped an inch at this mirage in the distance. Himself was coming towards him. He screwed up his eyes and, out of the shimmering haze behind this mirror image, rose three weird and wonderful figures. They looked like women but as they drew nearer, their stubbly chins and hairy chests swelling beneath their décolleté bodices gave hint of their masculinity. No-Voice shook his head. But the nightmare pressed on. By now Maddon was aware of this approaching vision.

'Fuck-a-double-duck,' quoted Maddon. 'There's two of you,' as Dead Eye Dick, on yet another daring mission in disguise, thundered past.

When the dust had settled, normality had returned to the desert and Dead Eye was but a fart on the horizon, No-Voice attempted to unscramble his once-cool brains. He had it in a trice. Mulling over what Maddon had told him, he realised that some forward chappie had been impersonating his person. And it was this bogus No-Voice who had obviously bungled the bank raid.

Now that he suddenly realised that he was wanted by the law, he had no desire to show himself in Gold Dust. He approached the outskirts of the town with great caution. Early morning was the busy time. Commerce was at its height. The townspeople rushed about on their daily grind.

No-Voice led the two horses around the back of the ice cream parlour, and almost bumped his head on a bulky air conditioning unit which hung at a precarious angle on the back wall. He undid the reins of his captive's steed and steered the beast out into the middle of the street. He crept after it and gave it a sharp slap on the rump which sent the horse careering out of control down the main drag. No-Voice was back in the saddle and off before anyone had even discovered his entry. He sighed at his departing bounty. That was one lot of dollars he'd have to go without. He didn't like it one bit.

But Clit did. She'd been out on the trail ever since she'd discovered Maddon had done a bunk. And she hadn't seen hide nor pube of him. And, hey presto, here was her enemy delivered to the door.

'Well, shiver my timbers,' she exclaimed in her broad cowboyese. 'Wells Fargo sure is providing one helluva service these days!'

Chapter Fourteen

A GAGGLE OF GOOLY GOBBLERS

Meanwhile, Lurex Tex had had yet another of her money-making brainwaves. She'd decided to take her particular show on the road. Leaving Hilda Burger in charge of the theatrical side of her business and Scarlet and Abe up-front in the fun-parlour, she'd decided mobile brothels were the thing of the future. And she'd be the first with the idea – around Gold Dust anyway. She'd designed a double-length, double decker waggon, which she'd got the local carpenters and sailmakers, Toulouse Lautrec and Son, to fashion for her. This extraordinary shaghouse-on-sixteen-wheels was the most bizarre vehicle ever to be seen in the west. It was about fourteen foot high. The first deck, which was divided into eight cubicles, had a wooden lid to it. Above that the other eight compartments were topped by a canvas roof. Back of the seat where the driver would sit was a rather spacious spot, which Tex would call her own. From this commodious room, Tex would be able to oversee all comings and goings. The most remarkable feature of this room was the enormous cash till, in which Tex hoped to store her dollars. She'd planned her route with care; all the outlying farms would be visited. And they would start at Webster's. She picked sixteen of her freshest tinsley tarts. They were all done up like Christmas trees for their excursion. Came the day when Tex and her travelling gangbang gaggle of gooly-gobblers were to leave town, even the Mayor of Gold Dust was out in the street to wish them Bon Screwing.

As the military band played 'I Was Born Under A Wandering Whore,' the flagship SS Goodtime steamed out and onto the trail.

The mobile brothel meandered off out of town, heading straight for Webster's ranch. Its rear view disappearing out of Gold Dust made a very odd picture indeed. The hazard warning signs on the back of the wandering fun-palace shouted at passing cowpokes. 'Left hand drive,' 'Caution: Fragile load,' 'Quiet, cowpokes fucking,' and 'French letters for sale – apply within.' At the front, Tex rode proudly while she ground the hand organ which played an appropriate tune – the unmelodious grating disturbed the desert air. It was Tex's favourite song of the moment and top of the Irish hit parade: 'Hit me with your shovel, Mick!'

It didn't take them long to reach the Websters. Tex felt sure there'd be at least a couple of customers here. She was wrong. Although the male flesh may have been willing, Mrs. Webster was not weak. The short scrawny woman shuffled out of the house like a sack of potatoes. She didn't have to look twice to realise what had driven up to her front door. Tex assumed she didn't approve from the menacing way she levelled her twelve bore and peppered the brand new waggon with shot. At the same time, she held the knob of the door, successfully blocking Webster Senior and Junior's passage to pleasure. Tex and crew didn't hang around to argue. There were plenty more cocks out there, after all, just busting for a bang. She put the waggon into reverse and turned turtle on the ranch.

The vehicle lumbered away, lurching along the track to its next port of call. Which was the saddlemakers. Bill and Ben were still recovering from their recent orgasms. They lay sprawled where No-Voice's sister had left them and their cocks were just about ready to face another erection; if Tex supplied the scaffolding . . . After organ-grinding for some considerable time to no avail – there was no sign of life – Tex went in to see where the hell the flower pot men had got to. There surely had to be custom here, so far from the easy delights of town.

'Shop,' lied Tex, as she burst into the craftsmen's front workroom.

Ben lay naked, legs akimbo on the floor. His clay pipe hung erotically from between his lips. Tex looked for his cock but couldn't see it anywhere. Bending down and peering closely, she managed to locate a tiny pink tip, as big as the top of her little finger. She groaned, and inwardly decided that this was not her lucky day. Tex's interest, however, must have spurred some interest in old Ben, and his little pinkie perked up to its mammoth inch-and-a-half proportions. She gave it an encouraging pat and passed on into the back room, enticed by brother Bill's sexy sighs. He was, at the time, lying flat on his back with his mouth wide open and snoring like a randy rhinoceros. She grabbed his horn and he came to immediately. Wiping the sticky goo from her hands, she enquired as to whether they wanted a fuck. The saddlers enthused and proceeded to give Tex the wad of notes that No-Voice had given them for the services they had rendered. The aged pair wanted to go through the whole gamut of Tex's staff. They hobbled out of their house and over the rough ground, kicking the odd chicken as they went, and managed to climb aboard the caravan of erotica. From room to room they went – each having started at opposite ends. With a shag, shag here and a wank, wank there, these two old Macdonalds whipped through Tex's farmyard. It took a day and a half before the two old boys met in the middle of the lower deck. And they were game to climb the stairs and start on the top deck, but Tex insisted that they'd already had their money's worth. With that, she kicked them off the back of the lorry and ordered the waggon train to move out. They were left as they'd been left before, prone on their pricks in the dirt.

The moving Madame decided to set up camp for the night, to give the travel-worn occupants of the fuck-truck a well-earned rest. Tex withdrew to her counting house and proceeded to amass the takings so far. Outside, the girls were rubbing sticks together in an effort to create a blaze to cook their supper. It took some time before the sparks began to fly. But soon they were sitting around a roaring camp fire. The coolie chef was busy stirring his bubbling cauldrons and their mouths watered as their knickers dried in the fierce heat. The menu was not particularly appetising, but it was certainly inventive. The first course was an exotic soup à la rattlesnake; just the thing to get your tastebuds frothing. The next delicacy set before them was Coyote Roti, which they complained bitterly about. It was, they said, as tough as old boots and not half as tasty. The coolie took no notice of their comments, mainly because he couldn't understand a word of English. He just smiled inanely at the man-eating mob. His piece de resistance was the sweet – Cockroach Surprise – which was actually simple cockroaches in jelly. The whores went berserk and several jellies sailed through the air like unmanned missiles. The coolie'd obviously had practice at avoiding the return of his own creations. He dodged adroitly all attacks on his person. Their cries of rage brought Tex out into the open. Her timing was bad. As her head appeared in the opening, she caught an aspic delight on her kisser. The sickly stuff gelled for a moment, quivered, and then slipped off her face and onto her protruding mammaries. The cockroaches, fed up with this inhuman treatment, flew off her chest in disgust.

Later, things had calmed down considerably and the coolie had been strung up by his balls. The girls were enjoying a little harmonising to the tune of Tex's organ when, over the hubbub, Tex heard the sound of several guns being cocked. She jumped to her feet as twelve men, guns drawn and at the ready, moved towards the jolly campers in a menacing circle.

'It's Buster Brick,' she breathed to the others.

Panic ensued, as the girls tried to reach the safety of their new home. The henchmen stopped their flight by firing warning shots in the air. The tarts screeched to a halt in a huddle at the back of the bangbus. A sea of hoods surged forward and the women were almost deafened by the noise of popping trouser buttons. The quick-witted, fast-footed Tex had, by this time, got her notes up her knickers and was lying under the waggon well out of sight. She could survey the scene from her vantage point and her eyes were met by shocking scenes of depravity. Big tears welled up in her eyes as she was forced to witness all this fucking for nothing. Protesting at first, the ladies, now, were strewn everywhere. The night air, which had earlier been full of anguished cries, was soon echoing with ecstatic whoops of wantonness. Two of the nightlights had their talons in Buster. He was sitting in a canvas chair with a name on the back while a head buried itself into his lap. His other girl busied herself by giving him a stranglehold around the neck. But he wasn't choking – he was licking as though his life depended on it. The girl in his groin was bobbing up and down like a cork on the sea. Buster straightened his legs, arched his back and thrust his rod further into the warm moist valley. Draped over one of the wheels of the waggon, was a long-legged thin shapely blonde. Her skirt had been hitched up to her neck and her French lace drawers were around her ankles. The spokes of the wheel pressed into her arse. Her knees trembled violently as a burly cowhand poked her savagely. His bottom muscles flexed like tight rope, as he worked furiously in and out of the girl's accommodating cunt. As he worked away hard, the girls feet left the ground and she was left speared to his cock and held by the cart. With a thundering roar, that almost knocked Tex's pride and joy vehicle over, the man came and came and came. The two gently fell to the sex-soaked floor, locked in each other's arms.

Over near the fire, dappled light flickering on their naked forms, another outlaw and his hooker were getting their rocks off. A small mean man had lain the floozie across his knees and was spanking her round neat bottom with his bare hand. The slaps reverberated around the clearing. His other hand was disappearing between her legs, as he brought her off in the most unusual way. By this time Tex was taking notes!

Elsewhere, a thickset roughneck was bending over a Botticelli, savouring her huge reddish brown nipples. Nearby, another couple were mutually masturbating. The tempting tart had a firm grip on the young man's fancy and was fondling his balls in a manner crazed. She had her head back and her eyes closed while he wanged her in earnest. A few yards away, one of Tex's team was hammering her ride into the ground. He had his large paws on her waist and was lifting her up and down, exposing inches of thick glistening meat on the upstroke. She whooped and yelled like an Indian on the warpath.

The rest of the coupling cavorters were engaged in a mind-fucking orgasmic frenzy. Tex lay under the wagon in great distress. All this come-come-dancing, and there she was, stuck like a wallflower with no partner at the ball. She couldn't stand it. She just had to leave this spunk-sodden arena and clear her head in the cool night air. She nipped out from under the waggon wheels, and walked carefully, so as not to dislodge the dough in her knickers, away from the clusterfuck. In a way, she was a mite upset that nobody noticed her going, so busy were they with their coming. Sniffing sadly to herself, she went her solitary way. Miles and miles and miles she plodded, deep in the depths of her despondency.

'How could they do it?' she sobbed. 'They could have made a mint for me out of that lot!'

Anger replaced her sorrow and she started to march she knew not where. Sunrise found her a wee wilted heap in the shade of a high rockface. She hadn't a clue where she was. Nor did she know where her bordello band was situated. She only knew that she had to have some water or she would die. Casting her eyes left, right and centre, she perceived all at once a clit in the rocks. Then recognition hit her between the tits. This craggy formation of rocks was part of the Superstition Mountain range. And perhaps there was water between the rocks. She stepped forward and peered into the cleft. It seemed to have no end. Her curiosity on the rise, she stumbled forward. Tex shivered at the sudden gloom that hit her, as she moved out of the sunlight. Cautiously, she inched down the passage in the granite. Like a painful old tortoise, she made her way into the heart of the stone. Coming to the end of the shadows, Tex was suddenly exposed to sunlight. She blinked like a new-born bat, as the strong shafts of light shafted her. Her pace quickened as the going became easier. Spurred on by the realisation that this hole was leading somewhere exciting, her heart thudded unnaturally in her breast. The tortoise in her sloughed off its shell and the hare in her leapt forward. She crossed the opening that she came to in the mountains. There was no way ahead, just vegetation sprouting, as though from the wall itself.

'Aha,' she thought suspiciously. 'A tree cannot have its roots in rock, there must be something behind it.'

She gingerly edged forward and plucked at the first scraggy branch. She let out a whistle of wonderment, as the bush pulled back to reveal a hidden entrance. She slipped through the opened curtain and passed down the path ahead. The tortuous winding pathway wound on for what seemed like miles. She gasped. There on the level ground in front of her stood a wooden shack. Beside the house was a corral where two horses grazed on horse fodder. She twitched with excitement as she recognised one of the animals. Surely the big white horse was the creature that The-Man-With-No-Voice had used when he'd brought Big Nose to justice. So, she had discovered No-Voice's lair. Hardly daring to breathe, she crept stealthily forward on the tips of her toes. Reaching the verandah, she froze in her tracks. Two huge luminous eyes above a curved vicious beak stared into hers! Their unblinking gaze mesmerised the confused conlady. Dragging her orbs from the fiery eyeballs, she surveyed the rest of the eagle's plumage. She despaired as she took in the creature's long sharp talons. But then she noticed, to her relief, that the big bird was securely tied to its perch. Not a sound could be heard from within the shack. So, ignoring the peculiar guard dog, Tex cautiously went up to a dirty window and pressed her nose to the pane. Completing her recce and satisfying herself that nobody lurked with intent in the interior, she placed a trembling hand upon the well-worn knob. It creaked as she turned it. The door swung back. She stepped over the threshold and into her doom . . .

Chapter Fifteen

CIRCUS TRICKS

Meanwhile, the citizens of Gold Dust had woken one morning to find that their walls had been covered with a rash of multi-coloured posters. They read: 'Bailey's Circus, the greatest show on earth will be coming to YOUR town soon, and presenting to an astonished public: lions, elephants, the ape-woman, the rat man, the only woman in the world with a beard, the daring Zenellis on the flying trapeze AND a hundred other spesh acts, including the astonishing unique Bella, the world's most famous contortionist. All on show from Friday May 13th to the 31st. Tickets obtainable from Tex's saloon bar. Hurry, hurry, folks. Don't miss this once-in-a-lifetime experience!'

These notices caused intense excitement. Apart from rustling and murder and hold-ups and occasional skirmishes with savages, and rapes and kidnapping and bank raids and bounty hunters bringing bare-arsed bounty, and suicidal sheriffs, not much happened in the old town. The children especially went nearly mad with excitement and pestered their mothers and fathers, until they drove them almost out of their minds. The butch young men were *blasé*, pretending to be disinterested but, whenever they thought nobody was looking, they would carefully examine the advertisements, paying particular attention to Bella! In her high boots, with her whip at the ready, she seemed to promise unmentionable delights to the eye. As May wore thin, talk increased and on the twelfth, the great Bailey Circus rode into town and booked the whole of Ma O'Shea's lodging house. Bailey himself was accompanied by a gorgeous young woman with fair hair and violet eyes. Together, they strolled around town, inspecting sites for the big top.

Hilda Burger, enjoying her stint as an impressario, had double booked. She'd sent for the circus, quite forgetting that she already had a permanent show in town. So crazed with power was Hilda, that she insisted that the tent go next to the theatre in Tex's herb garden. The canvas enveloped the building. It seeped in through doors and windows like squidgy marshmallow. The tent pole went straight into Miss Allsorts' cunt – she was practising her pas de deux at the time – and out the other side. She hardly felt a thing. Having realised the enormity of her mistake, Miss Burger told the circus to fuck off. They eventually chose a square plot of land just north of town. On the 13th, the townspeople leapt out of bed to find that, in the night, twelve huge horsedrawn brilliantly-coloured caravans had arrived. Giant pegs were being driven into the ground, whilst burly men laboured with ropes.

On the same day, Bella arrived, in the following manner: A black horse, foaming with sweat, suddenly dashed into the main street and its vivid rider, in a dark brown riding habit, jumped off its back and strode straight into the saloon. Her black hair flowed behind her loosely held in a scarlet ribbon. Black eyes flashed out of a faultless face flushed by her exercise. Calmly, she took stock of all the men present. She spat on the ground, looking them up and down as though she could see through their clothes. Then she stared boldly into their eyes, as if evaluating their penile worth. At last her glance fell on Chuck Carson and, attracted by the star, she glided up to his table and sat on his knee.

'Champagne please,' she cooed in his ear.

Chuck, in a bemused way, beckoned to Abe to fetch one of the few bottles in the house. This would take care of the pocket money Rose had given him out of the housekeeping.

'Well, do you know who I am?' asked the lady.

Chuck, who had begun to recover his composure, replied: 'I guess you are Bella. Your pictures are plastered all over our little town.' Puffing his cock up proudly, he continued: 'I'm the deputy sheriff of this place. You probably guessed.'

'I had,' she replied brightly, and added with a smile: 'Why, otherwise, did you think I'd be interested in your body?'

Bella slipped off Chuck's lap, casually brushing his hardness as she went. She lowered herself seductively onto the chair beside him and stared insolently at the grit in his groin. Even Chuck had to blush at this forward, out-of-town approach. For a moment, the woman's gall made him wonder if this couldn't be his lady rapist. She had the same bold affrontry, certainly. While he was thus musing, he felt pressure upon his prick. Bella had a leg up and was pushing the sole of her tight ankle-hugging leather boot into his privates on parade. All the while, she sipped her wine delicately, as if nothing was happening at all. Her other foot was hell bent on snaking its way up one of his trouser legs. She massaged the bulge of his calf with her instep. Rose ruined this budding romance. Crash! Chuck found the champagne cork up his bum. This gentle hint from Rose reminded him of his nuptials. He left. And Bella turned her attentions elsewhere, to the unfortunate Sheriff Rosen, who just happened in behind his star.

It is no exaggeration to say, that the whole town was in love with Bella. After that first day, they all adored her. And strange as it may seem, even the women liked her. Ma O'Shea put a quilted cover on her bed which hadn't been out of the cupboard for ten years. Such an honour. But Bella was not happy. She confided in Ma O'Shea that directly she hit a new town, she wanted a new man. And she usually found one. Not this time, however. Were there no hidden beautiful young men? Ma thought immediately of Matthew. He certainly had a fine featured face and nice big cock. But he was Clit's steady. Nevertheless she mentioned him to Bella.

'Ask him,' said the contortionist, 'to a private show we are putting on tonight.'

Matthew received his invite and thought carefully as to

whether or not he should go. However, Clit had been away for a few days, escorting Jake Maddon to the county jail. He decided, therefore, to take up with Bella. The preview was shown to Sheriff Rosen, the bank manager, the Mayor and about twenty prominent men and their wives. The whip cracked. The lions obeyed. The clowns tumbled. The elephants roared. The freaks freaked out. And by eleven o'clock, Bailey had said goodbye to the last of his guests. As Matthew was about to go, Bella came up looking exceedingly lovely and asked him to stay and watch the Zenelli's rehearse. Bailey said goodnight and left. The tent was almost in darkness. Then Bella lit the lanterns and pointed them upwards. Matthew saw two Zenellis stark naked on either side of the ring on elevated perches. Madame Zenelli was the first to move. She hung by her arms, gently swinging. Then, Zenelli himself started to swing and Matthew could see that he had an enormous cockstand. The two swung nearer to each other, then Madame Z changed position. She hung with her knees over the bar and her head downwards. They flew closer and closer, until she could reach out and take his cock firmly in her mouth. Back and forward they went, joined together, until at last she let him go and they both sat resting on their opposite bars.

Soon they were off again. This time Madame Z had her legs open and her partner had put on a contraption that made his cock stick straight out. They got nearer and nearer. He aimed his cock at her but it failed to stick. They fell apart. The next time, he swung harder and entered her as she brought her legs together and transferred her arms to his trapeze, all in one deft movement. So they stayed, for perhaps five minutes. Glued together, dangling in mid-air. Then they parted and climbed down to the ground. They crossed to Bella, who congratulated them on their dirty feat. Matthew looked down to see what she was talking about.

With her eyes shining, she turned to Matthew: 'Wasn't that a magnificent sight? To see them fucking high in the sky?'

He nodded, his knob straining and bucking in his drawers. Bella looked at the movement between his legs and laughed.

'Ready for one are you?' she asked innocently, while pressing her warm body against his.

She could feel the heat and hardness of his fleshy tool through the layers of her clothing. Matthew was ripe for plucking; Bella, wet at the crotch.

'Will you go up?' she asked the horny young man.

Hanging from his legs from the narrow bar, Matthew wished he'd never said yes to her last question. Bella was sitting on the bar opposite, wearing a broad smile and absolutely nothing else. Her naked legs dangled. Her naked toes pointed elegantly. Matthew had an upside-down view of the wondrous woman's open sex. It was, to him, a pink slit of soft perfection. All at once, it was on the move. Matthew almost fell from his precarious perch, as the oncoming cunt became larger and larger before his very eyes. He raised himself up to meet the widening crack. Pubes brushed against his face. He caught the musky scent of her pussy and then she was gone again; winging her way back across the ring under the dark canvas of the big top. Matthew's vertigo vanished, as his cock roused itself once again. His prick ached with anticipation. Thoughts of another Clit were gone from his reeling sex-sodden brain. She came at him again and he could feel her body heat as she touched against him. His breath was escaping in hoarse rapid busts. Desperation flooded through him in great waves. He had to have her – but how could he get at her, so far from the ground? Bella provided the answer to this six dollar question by flinging herself at him the next time she sailed through the air on the flying trapeze. For a second, she slithered past and Matthew thought he had lost her. But their hands locked fast together. Thus he stayed suspended by his arms. Her very presence made him feel within a razor's edge of orgasm. If he came now, his spunk would spray like an angry geyser into thin air. He was pondering this problem, when she sprang like a jack in the box and coiled her smooth legs around his thighs. He'd forgotten she was a contortionist. Her pussy sat upon his face. Matt pushed back the folded plump lips of her cunt with his tongue. He drank deeply, savouring every drop of her rare and wonderful love juice. His hands itched to stroke her smooth hairless body. And now she was supporting herself with the vice-like grip of her thighs, Matthew's hands reached out for her. The feel of her made his pulses race. Blood was rushed to the head of his tool. His cock jerked forward instinctively. This wild movement between his thighs caused Matthew to become unbalanced. His legs lost their hold and suddenly cock, balls, pussy and boobs were plunging downwards towards the deck. Matthew thought his end had come. Terminal climax! His life flashed before him. Thoughts zoomed through his brain. What would Clit say when he was eventually found in this compromising position with Bella? As Matthew prayed for a quick painless end or a miracle, he found himself bouncing like a rubber ball in the safety net. Bella's legs and arms were all over him. He felt as though he was in the grip of a sex-mad octupus. Her large boobs jiggled up and down, squashing into his face. Finally, they lay still, recovering their breath in the comforting cradle of netting. They reached across and felt each other. Bella caught hold of Matt's hand and pressed it down between her legs. He could feel how wet she was. While he dallied there, she curled her fingers around his thickening stalk. Matthew's poor penis was somewhat puzzled at having been up and down like an aerobatic yo-yo. One minute on the point of coming; the next, scared out of its wits and lifeless. Now within ten feet of solid earth, it felt it could rise with safety. It came up with the swiftness of a souffle. Bella sighed contentedly as it grew in her grasp. She started a slow steady milking action. Matthew lay back, his fingers dipping in and out of her hot-pot. He felt bold enough now to speak and asked her, would she like his throbbing cock right up inside her. She answered pleasantly enough:

'Fuck me.'

The fun started.

Matthew moved his body over her stationary form, his heavy-duty fuck muscle above her shimmering twat. He lunged forward and his thrust set the net bouncing and he missed her by miles, his cock hammering eventually through a gap in the net. He came to rest with a painful twang against his balls. Bella who had closed her eyes to wait for the magnificent entry, opened them again to discover Matthew's sorry plight. She pulled him to her and he came out of the netting making a noise like a cork being plucked from a bottle. They bounced around for a while, then came to rest together. This time, Matthew took much more care and much more time with his entry into wonderment. He slowly eased his length into her, encountering no problems this time with the super bouncey bed they had chosen for their fuck. She gave an animal moan of sheer joy, as his long length beavered its way up her love tube. She knotted her legs firmly around his back, as if the couple needed more fuck adhesive to keep their bodies together. Now, when he jumped, she jumped with him. He banged her into the netting and it gave under the impact, sending the coupling couple high in the sky. On the descent, Matthew's cock went even further into the deep throat of her pussy. She clung to him, glued, forever impaled upon his sharp weapon. And so they fucked, flung around and around, up and down, by the elastic netting. They sailed skyward and came to earth. She carried her steed in this amazing matrimony of flesh upon flesh. His tongue drew out hers. He sucked the pointed serpent deep into his mouth. Their coming seemed to go on forever, echoing around the cavernous canvas. And when he had spewed the last of his spew into her and she had sucked the very last dribble from him, they stopped moving and lay in a steamy heap . . .

It was the early hours of the morning when they staggered back to Ma O'Shea's boarding house. Here, Matthew took the beauteous Belle again. They thrashed about with such vigour that the bed clothes fell off the bed, into a heap on the floor. The bed creaked and strained under the weight and movement, and the headboard thumped an urgent tattoo upon the ageing plaster. This and the piercing screams of Bella roused, not only the occupants of the next room, but everyone in the lodging place. Mister O'Shea, whose tool had stiffened at the sounds from down the hall, reached across to the sleeping form next to him and searched tentatively between his wife's plump thighs. Ma O'Shea snored contentedly, while Bella, in the next-room-but-one, screamed her lust. Paddy O'Shea's thick fingers entered his wife's matronly cunt in answer. An army could mount her, he thought, and she wouldn't know until she woke up in a puddle of spunk next morning. Bella was shrieking by now and the walls shuddered with the impact of the fucking bed. The sounds of slapping flesh reached a crescendo and even Ma O'Shea muttered in her sleep, as her husband thrust away at her wide pouch, sharing in the rising peaks of excitement from the room along the corridor. In the farthest corner of the house, the sounds could be heard too. The atmosphere was electric. Its current flowed from room to room, charging spent sexual batteries of those who had fucked earlier and exhausted themselves. Here and there, began the rhythms of more lovemaking. A symphony of sound – sighing and moaning and then sharpening mounting passion as young women milked their men with hands and cunts. The maidens sighed and stretched and pressed their thighs together. Old men at their portals abused themselves shamelessly. And then, as suddenly as it had begun, the noise subsided like a passing mistral. Doors closed, beds were quiet and the boarding house went back to sleep. Mister O'Shea panted, as semen seeped from his stalk. And his wife snored on . . .

Chapter Sixteen

AN UNBELIEVABLE CLIMAX

Meanwhile, Tex, tits trembling, tore into the cabin she'd found and was blasted by a pungent wall of orange blossom. No-Voice's women obviously had no taste, thought Tex, almost gagging on the cheap and nasty scent. She surveyed the one room of the shack, looking for definite clues as to the character of the inhabitants. She was surprised to find that the home lacked any sort of feminine influence. She was faced by a heavy, sparse, masculine domain. The one female touch was the ornate silver mirror that stood on a table. How could three women have their base here with the bounty hunter? And yet leave so little trace of their existence? Where on earth did they all sleep? The room boasted one small narrow cot only! Did they all curl up there together? But they couldn't possibly, unless they were stacked one on top of another. Her thirst forgotten, she poked around as only nosey people do. She rummaged under the bed and took the room apart systematically. Finally, she came upon the large chest that sat majestically on the floor. She tried in vain to prize the lid open. The lock was firm and resisted her advances. Desperate to get a gander inside and learn the secret of the locked box, Tex looked maniacally around for a key. She hunted high and low but could find it nowhere. Whilst prying into No-Voice's business, the super-sleuth found, high up in the wooden wall, the bounty hunter's bounty. A niche in the boarding fell away at her delicate touch to reveal thousands of crisp new banknotes. She toyed with the idea of grabbing the loot and running off with it. But thirst and her curiosity overcame her. She poured a deep draught of water from the jug on the table and gulped it back greedily. During this time, her women's intuition had been working overtime. She was firmly convinced that the chest would provide the answer to No-Voice's mysterious persona. She went outside to look for something sharp and pointed, with which to pick the lock. Her eyes lit upon the eagle's beak. Surely the giant bird would make mincemeat of the metal fastener. So thinking, she bent to untie the creature's tether. Talking softly into the feathers, she undid first one knot, then the other. The bird cocked its head to one side and gave her an inquisitive look. The creature remained as mute as its master, as Tex put out her arm to support the roc. It flapped its wings and descended gently onto her bare forearm. With this giant feathered attachment fastened to her person, Tex could hardly stumble her way back into the shack. The very size of the thing made it difficult – exceedingly difficult – to navigate the small opening. In a flurry of feathers, the unlikely pair gained entry.

'Good birdee,' said Tex patting it on the head.

With no more ado, she dumped it on the floor beside the chest and pointed at the lock. She carried on chatting to it, as all people talk to dumb animals.

'Peckie, peckie poo,' she cooed, frantically trying to persuade the bird to take more of an interest in the chest's lock. Its beady eyes stared balefully at the coaxing Tex. It was obvious that it didn't understand a word she was saying. Exasperated at the bird's stupidity, she grabbed its head between her hands and, using its beak like a hammer, attacked the uncooperative lock. Aghast at this treatment, Ernie the Eagle let out an unearthly eerie gurgling sound from deep within its throat. It had just started to fight back, when the lock snapped and the lid of the chest flew open. Tex caught a brief glimpse of three wigs sitting on piles of delicate lace women's clothing. The red, blonde and black hairpieces flashed before her eyes, as she was dragged unceremoniously along the floor of the wooden shack. Before she knew what was happening, her head hit the side of the door, bounced off and was slammed down the steps of the house and across the verandah. Her body followed along with it! The eagle had its claws in her. Excited by the sudden movement of the chest lid, Ernie had attempted maiden flight. He had been slightly restricted by the low ceiling of the building and, in his aerobatic attempt to reach lift-off, had become entangled in Tex's elaborate costume. He'd headed for the door dragging her with him and they now lay in a sea of plumes in the dirt outside. To Tex's further surprise, her ordeal was only just starting . . . Ernest repositioned his talons and grabbed Tex's shoulders firmly. Her ankles grazed the gate of the corral, as he ascended to the heavens. She couldn't believe this was happening to her. What a day it was turning out to be! By this time, they had reached five hundred feet and the shack below looked the size of a matchbox. After the initial shock of her recent blast off, Tex was, by now, recovering her meagre senses. She took time out to enjoy her flight of fancy. Ernie appeared to be heading deep into the scraggy peaks of the Superstition Mountains.

'God,' she thought, 'I'm going to be up a peak without a paddle if I don't do something to rectify my position immediately.'

She looked around frantically for straws to clutch. And spotted a talon . . .

'Ahh, his rudder,' she thought, giving it a sharp exploratory tug.

The winged beast responded immediately and veered off and back in the direction of Gold Dust. This was just what she'd hoped for. If she could persuade her feathered friend to descend into town, she'd be able to come down like a bolt from the blue with the whereabouts of No-Voice's hideaway on her lips. Tex's life, however, was not as simple as this. The recalcitrant bird, with a mind and beak of its own, did a couple of flypast circles over town. As hard as she pulled on its talons, she could not get the eagle to alter his haphazard flight-path. Suddenly, the crazy Ernie took off at alarming speed in an easterly direction. By the time the flying whore had taken off for airspace new, a considerable crowd of rubber-necking inhabitants had gathered in the Gold Dust street. Now, where was the misguided missile heading?

Tex didn't have long to wait for the answer. The cruising couple were soon hovering over a ramshackle rundown derelict and falling-apart ranch. She hadn't a clue whose it was. As if reading her thoughts, the bird took a beak dive for the ground. Tex's stomach lurched at this speedy change in altitude. The irregular descent caused her ears to pop wildly, like corn. Just before they hit, the intelligent Ernie slowed right down and levelled off. Inch by inch the bird winged over the tumbledown homestead. Tex could see it clearly now – and the four figures that were clowning around on the verandah. The three ugly and mis-shapen men were forcing their ungainly bodies into women's clothes. But it was the fourth man, or dick, that caught her eye. There was no mistaking that cock. That was the cock of The-Man-With-No-Voice. She remembered it well – the night he'd burst into her bordello and ravished her on the spot and on the bed and on Fatso. Just then, her No-Voice copped an eyeful of the eagle. He looked up and screamed in horror at the approaching winged weirdos.

'Fuck a duck,' expleted Dead Eye Dick, for that's who it really was.

'Fuck an eagle more like,' screamed the now-thin Fatso, running for the cover of the house. There he took up his favourite hiding position, under the bed.

Tex took in this scene and was confused. No-Voice had spake. But No-Voice wasn't supposed to be able to speak. But that cock, that poncho, that cigar and that sombrero belonged to the man she loved. A terrible thought struck her. She had been duped. And what was worse, fucked by an imposter. This was Dead Eye Dick, the desperate bandito. She recognised him now from the wanted posters in the sheriff's office.

'I love you,' she screamed, as the eagle took off again.

She waved her legs in a gesture of farewell and gave Dick more than a glimpse of her flying saucer.

'Tex,' yelled the criminal. 'Come back, my love. Where are you going?'

'I wish the bloody hell I knew,' she returned.

And then the distance was too far for their telecommunications to reach. Dick threw himself into his breeches and threw himself onto his horse. He galloped after the disappearing birds, who were now heading straight back for Gold Dust again. He rode as straight as the crow flies and bumped into several cacti. Pricking himself up from these spikey encounters, he carried on undaunted by these minor setbacks. He was in love. His head was full of violins. And that was about all.

Ernie and Tex arrived back at town before Dead Eye. The bird found a hot air thermal and circled effortlessly around and around Gold Dust. Again cries were taken up in the streets below.

'Look, look, it's Tex,' screeched a hysterical Hilda Burger, waving her willie warmers skyward.

'Come down Tex,' they screamed.

But Ernest didn't heed their cries. He just went right on circling. Tex, who had never seen Gold Dust from this vantage point before, began surveying the rooftops with interest.

'Oh, there,' she thought pointing pointlessly at the hole in the roof of her fun-parlour, 'is Miss Allsorts sun bathing. And in the nude again.'

She peered closer for a better look and was dismayed to see that the very large hole was not any part of Clitoris' anatomy but a nasty crack in her building. Before she had time to sort that intricate little problem out, her attention was grabbed by the huge letters, sewn in Miss Hilda Burger's handwriting, on the top of a large strange-shaped tent, pitched just outside of town.

'Tex's Big Top!' it screamed.

The fact that the circus had come to town was surprise enough for the poor girl. But what her big top was doing there when it should have been up here with her, she had no idea. Ernest decided that he's had enough of this particular view and roared off back in the direction of the Superstitions. Tex's cries of 'Help, help, save me,' and words to that effect, were lost in the rush of wind. She realised all was lost.

Anything could happen to her now. Where was this big bird going? The best thing she could do was to try to communicate with those on the ground, the position of No-Voice's lair. This she could do at least . . . even if her life could not be spared. Taking her eyebrow pencil from behind her ear, where she always kept it for just such an emergency as this, she whipped off her open-crotch pantaloons. With great difficulty, she drew a rough sketch map detailing where to find the gap in the wall which lead to No-Voice's hidehole. She gesticulated like a lunatic to the people below and promptly dropped her pink funcovers. They fluttered slowly to the ground catching, before they reach terra firma, on a flagpole and got caught up in the stars and stripes.

Ernest winged on, overshooting No-Voice's camp and flew directly for the highest peak of the Superstitions. Tex's heart raced in her breast as the air got thinner and thinner and the ground got further and further away. Ernie flapped on. And just at that precise wank in time a free fall parachutist almost collided with the pair. Tex breathed a sigh of relief as they escaped yet another hazard of the air.

She was beginning to think that she had as many lives as a cat, when the eagle let go. This was it, she thought. Her end was nigh. But then her feet struck something solid. Dead Eye Dick's head. The love-sick bandit had followed her. His ropes and crampons jangled madly from his belt.

'Thank God I've found you in time,' he breathed, clicking his big sexy mountaineers boots.

As the two lovebirds caught up on recent experiences, Ernie returned to his perch and his agitated master.

Tex explained to Dead Eye how she'd stumbled onto No-Voice's secret place and Dick told her that it had indeed been him who had impersonated the bounty hunter and attempted the Gold Dust bank raid. They melted like ice cream in summer into each others arms. The ledge Tex had landed on, and Dead Eye had had such difficulty in getting to was narrow and hard. But so much in lust they were, that they didn't notice. But Tex did notice her would-be rescuer's condition. The man was in a pitiful state. His shirt hung in tattered remnants around his bruised and scratched torso. The remains of his trousers were sitting on his socks. His poncho and sombrero had been left miles back and with it his impersonation of No-Voice. His boots were scuffed beyond repair and belief.

They lunged at each other. Hot kisses rained down on Dead Eye's blackened face. Dick slipped his hand up Tex's dress, searching for her "start" button' He was excited to find that she's opened her thighs and the road to her panting pussy. He continued his exploration and placed a finger up her crack. He felt the tight elasticity of her cunt. This manipulation drove Tex to the point of no return.

'Take me,' she wheezed.

He thrust his fuck muscle into her delicate rosebud mouth and she gobbled it ravenously. The shaft took on an even more steel-like appearance, as it inched its sensual way down her throat. Fancying a bit of the other, he pulled back and thrust his member into the deep vee between her breasts. This was after wrenching her bodice down. He grabbed two handfuls and squashed them inwards on his raging erection. His body moved down as her skirts moved up and he explored the outer rim of her cunt with his fingers. Tex was prone on the pebbles. She reached for his vertical dong before it could make its final move. She lovingly teased the monster with thumb and forefinger. It sent him almost as high in passion as she'd been taken by the eagle. He lowered his fuckworm into her earthy hole. The rotation of rudes to rudes. The meshing and entwining of hairs. The sexual smells mingling with the clear mountain air. Dick began his shafting, humping away to his heart's content. Tex looked down and watched the pink cock disappearing from view behind her tuft of silken curls. Dick lowered himself onto Tex's hot squirming body, allowing his full weight to rest on her. His mouth found hers and their tongues meshed in an earth-shattering kiss. She licked and sucked his lips, then ran her fingers down his masculine back until she reached the rise of his buttocks. She parted her legs until she thought she would split in half under the force of his penetration. Never once did he jerk or thrust too violently. Just long meaningful lengths of love.

In mid-fuck, Tex whispered in his ear: 'All this time I've been fantasising over No-Voice, when all the while it was your wonderful bursting big one that I was hankering after. It's the best dick, Dick. And I've had some dicks in my time. Long, short, fat, thin, pointed, bent, bulbous, flat-headed, two-eyed, shovel-shaped – all have been where you are now. I was only interested in dicks before, now all I'm interested is Dick.'

Dead Eye was turned on by Tex's experience and the thrill of knowing that, with all the dickery that had gone up her cunt before, she had now chosen his. He screamed her name to the tors and shuddered as the rumblings of a volcano started in the base of his fat stalk. The vibrations escalated and he quaked as rivulets of passion surged through his veins. He came, spurting his lust-leak way into her womb. As the first drops hit the bullseye, Tex erupted too. She came. And the railroad was coming . . . They lay clawing each other in the frenzied throes of final orgasm.

They picked themselves up from the ledge, sponged the sweat of their labour of love from their bodies and looked around for a way of getting the fuck off this mountain. They followed the ledge around the side of a crag, discovering that it appeared to lead nowhere and especially not down. Tex, pissed off that the path lead nowhere, leant against the wall. It crumbled under her weight and she fell backwards into a hollow behind. Dick looked around to see his loved one disappearing up a crack. Picking debris from her legs, he followed on after her. They found themselves in a high-ceilinged cave. It took a while for their eyes to become accustomed to the gloom, but when their optics focused, they couldn't believe them. The wall directly in front of them was a solid seam of gold. From floór to roof the precious stuff glinted at them. At the foot of the gold precipice was a large pile of heavy nuggets. Quite forgetting their lust for one another, they raced for the goodies. A spade hung on a hook in the wall and alongside, a pick. The two gold-crazed people juggled nuggets, whooping for joy as they did so.

'Well, I'll be darned,' said Tex. 'Another little secret of The-Man-With-No-Voice. That's why the eagle flew me up here. It had been trained to do that. No-Voice couldn't possibly work the mine without ornithological assistance.'

This last utterance had completely confused Dick – he wasn't much of a bird fancier.

Then the awful truth dawned on them. They were rich beyond Tex's wildest dreams but, what good was money when you're alone on a shelf?

Dick shouted: 'I got up, so we must be able to get down. Just fill your knickers with nuggets and we'll be on our way.'

Alarmed by this macho-ness, it was then that Tex noticed that, not only had she disposed of her knickers earlier, but Dick's mountaineering equipment was nowhere to be seen either. His ropes and crampons had vanished, while they'd been loosing the lust from their loins. What were they to do? Jump?

No-Voice came home to find his bird had flown. Alarmed, he studied the tethers on the perch. They hadn't been broken by the force of the bird's strength, but untied by devious human hands. Who would have interfered with such a dangerous creature? A rush of wind and the flapping of wings made the mystified man whirl around. His pet was just coming into land. It taxied in and swung its under-carriage onto the perch, on the porch.

If the bird had been unleashed, thought No-Voice, it could well have taken the interloper off to his mine. There was no time to lose. They might have run off with his nuggets. With great elan, No-Voice tugged at the bird's tootsies. Ernie got the message – he was about to make another trip.

Off they soared.

Armed with Tex's panti-map, Clit was the first of the townspeople to reach No-Voice's hiding place. They missed each other by seconds and the ranch had an eerie stillness about it, as Clit clopped up on Brasso. She quickly discovered that the joint was empty. So she sat in the rocking chair on the verandah and waited for the return of the man she so desired to meet.

Ernie and friend landed on the ledge just minutes after taking off. The bird leapt off No-Voice and the latter passed quickly around to the entrance of the golden cave. As he came to the hole, he felt a right gooseberry. There, with her skirts pulled up over her head was Tex. Her naked arse stared him in the face. Very gently, Dead Eye Dick reached forward, unaware of the peeping Thomas and bird. He put a finger up her honeypot, as if exploring the fragile petals of a hothouse plant. She leant forward onto the shovel, apparently unconcerned and noticed two bright blue pairs of eyes staring into the gloom.

Tapping Dick on the shoulder, she cried 'Look.'

Dick dropped his hand from her hot twat and spun on his mountain boots to face the new arrivals. No-Voice stepped in menacingly.

'Ah, 'tis Long John Silver with his parrot.'

No-Voice, without a word as was his habit, bashed the two head's heads together and knocked them unconscious. Whilst they were in the land of painful nod, No-Voice got busy. Minutes later, he had tied Tex and Dick together face-to-face. He then lashed them to the giant bird of prey. He only used one of Ernie's legs, saving the other for his own ride down the mountain. Mercifully, the two trussed chickens did not recover consciousness until Ernest had completed a rather hazardous and lopsided touchdown. He came in like a Boeing with a lost engine. Clit had dozed off in the rocking chair but came to on hearing an amazing kerfuffle in the air.

The sight of this demented foursome, speeding towards her, caused her some consternation. But the quick-witted Clit soon took control, whipping out her six-shooter and pointing it at No-Voice – the man of her wet dreams.

With a bump, the quartet was down! Clit moved in. Covering No-Voice with her raised weapon, she quickly cut the ropes that held Dick and Tex. They fell on the floor in a heap and immediately starting fucking. Clit turned her attentions on No-Voice. She marched him into the shack, feeling for the lump between his legs as she went. Tex had told her so much about this man's big cock and yet, as she fumbled there, she couldn't see what all the fuss was about – she couldn't find an engorged pimple let alone a pulsating prick. The marshall's fumblings drove No-Voice into the shack in double-quick time. He wanted to get away from her pushy fingers. Once inside, Clit backed her prisoner onto the bed. She almost fainted. The smell of orange blossom almost knocked her senseless.

'How could he wear anything quite so sweet, cloying and feminine to boot?' She looked puzzled.

But she was determined to relieve the hot desire nestling in her knickers. Her gynaecology was on the warpath. Tex breezed over to The-Man-With-No-Voice and ordered him to strip. He froze and then shook his head with fervour. So, he was going to be uncooperative, thought Clit.

'I'll blow your balls off then,' she menaced, nudging her six inches of steel into his pelvic area.

He continued shaking his head, with horror in his eyes. Clit had had enough of this silly game. She marched over to him and slashed her way through his famous poncho. It fell like cheese through a grater onto the floor. Beneath he wore a loose fitting check shirt, tucked into black trousers. Clit raised the barrel of her gun and hooked it into the collar of his baggy shapeless shirt. She yanked. He screamed. A perfectly-formed milky breast fell exposed to Clit's view. She fainted.

Needless to say, when the ravaging hordes from Gold Dust

arrived on the scene, they were able to unravel the mysteries of the No-Voice saga. They found the eagle having his solitary end-away, Clit unconscious, No-Voice exposed, and Tex and her new-found love, Dick, rolling in a dustcloud of ecstacy.

The-Man-With-No-Voice was exposed as having been a woman all along. Why had she taken this role? Popular opinion felt that she – Kate Calamity – had adopted a man's character because the Wild Wild West was no place for a woman alone. A female bounty hunter was unheard of. The reason behind her role-swapping madness was, however, soon made clear. Kate was really a nun-loving Christian and all her bounty and the gold from the mountains, she'd dutifully taken each month to the nearby Mission House at San Miguel. She'd been their sole benefactress for years.

Once this horrendous mish-mash was cleared up, love and lust blossomed everywhere. Chuck and Rose had triplets – Chuck was made sheriff and Rose became headmistress of the local school. Hilda threw away her burger and became Mrs. Rosenberg. And the former sheriff Rosen followed his new wife into showbusiness. They became manager and manageress of Tex's little empire. Tex, meanwhile, concentrated her life on Dick. Not a great change, except that this was one particular Dick, of the Dead Eye variety! And Matthew, fresh from Bella's trapeze, fell desperately in love with Kate Calamity, who was able to put the bounty hunting behind her. Clit, being career-minded, rode off over the horizon into the sunset and onto much greater escapades.

The pathetic shanty town of Gold Dust, meanwhile, thanks to the legendary gold in No-Voice's mine, boomed like no boom had ever boomed before.

As the hacks flooded onto the set and flashers began popping indiscriminately, the actors, actresses and extras relaxed for the first time in weeks. Hollywood's premier blue movie company had another success on its hands . . .

IN DEPTH

Fiona Richmond

Fiona's wildest bestseller to date!

Miss Georgie Deuce has only two ambitions in life: success as a super-reporter and mind-blowing pleasure as a super-lover. But not necessarily in that order.

So when she's sent on her first assignment (she code-names it 'Around the World in Eighty Lays') and finds herself on a personal, first-hand, in-depth investigation into jet-set sex from Amsterdam to Bangkok, everything seems to be coming together very nicely.

But then, with Georgie, it usually does.